CARDAMOM SONGS

Original Norwegian title: Folk og røvere i Kardemomme by
first published in 1955 and in 1980 in a revised edition with new illustrations
by J.W. Cappelens Forlag a·s, Oslo
Copyright © Thorbjørn Egner 1955, 1980
English edition: When the Robbers Came to Cardamom Town
first published in 1993 by J.W. Cappelens Forlag a·s, Oslo
English translation: Copyright © Anthony Barnett 1993
Reprinted, with corrections, 1994

Typescript by Heien Fotosats A.s, Spydeberg
Printed by Livonia Print, Latvia 2017

ISBN 978-82-02-13977-3

11. opplag 2017

THORBJØRN EGNER

WHEN THE ROBBERS CAME
TO CARDAMOM TOWN

TRANSLATED FROM THE NORWEGIAN BY
ANTHONY BARNETT

ILLUSTRATED BY
THE AUTHOR

CAPPELEN DAMM

CHAPTER ONE—ABOUT POLICE INSPECTOR BASTIAN, OLD TOBIAS, AUNT SOPHIA AND OTHER FINE FOLK OF CARDAMOM TOWN

Cardamom is only a little town, and it lies so far away that almost nobody knows about it. Just you and me and a very few others.

Cardamom is a rather remarkable town, and a lot happens there that doesn't happen anywhere else. For example, donkeys and camels walk about in the streets, and even an elephant or two comes ambling along—now and then.

Old Tobias with his long white beard lives in the town, and the pork butcher and Puddleson the tram driver and Patterson the barber—and Remo and Tommy and Aunt Sophia and little Camomilla. As well as Police Inspector Bastian, the Superintendent, who never wants to arrest anyone. When he goes on his short beat through the town, he gives a friendly wave to the left and to the right and makes sure that everyone is doing fine.

POLICE INSPECTOR BASTIAN

I am Superintendent Bastian
and am a friendly man,
for I think a man should be that if he can.
And I walk about and see that all
are happy and are free,
for I think that is how everyone should be.

I have made up a law for Cardamom
and posted it around.
And in this law the following words are found:
You shall never bother others,
you shall be both fair and kind,
and whatever else you do I shall not mind.

In the middle of Cardamom Town stands a tall round house. This is Old Tobias's tower house. He is the wisest of all in the little town, which could be because he has such a long beard.

Among other things, he keeps an eye on the weather in Cardamom Town. With his long telescope he sits high up in his tower house peering out over the world. And when he sees a storm approaching in the distance he goes out onto the platform beside his room and calls out across the town square: "Hallo hallo—here is the weather forecast for this afternoon: Wet and windy conditions!" Then out come mackintoshes and galoshes and umbrellas, and when the rain comes nobody is caught out.

But even Tobias makes mistakes, and it's not so easy to know *everything* about the wind and the rain. One day, as he sat up in his tower house peering out, he saw heavy black clouds with sheets of rain below, far away in the east. He hurried out onto the platform and sent out a gale warning across the town: "Hallo hallo—here is the weather forecast for this afternoon: Easterly gales and heavy rain!"

"O huff o huff!" said the townsfolk and they rushed home to fetch umbrellas and mackintoshes. And anyone who had washing hanging on the line hurried to bring it in, even if it was still damp.

But while all this was going on the wind veered, and the clouds sailed off in quite another direction and didn't come anywhere near Cardamom Town. People walked along holding their umbrellas and looking up at the sky. "Isn't it going to rain, then, soon?" they asked. But the rain didn't come. Many of them felt cross and complained: "Old Tobias has made a fool out of us today."

Not one drop of rain fell that day. But the next day Old Tobias again observed black, threatening clouds far away in the east. They were headed straight for Cardamom Town. "There's no doubt about it this time," Tobias said to himself, and he hurried out onto the platform and called out over the town: "Here is the weather forecast for this afternoon: Easterly gales and heavy rain!"

But then Patterson the barber and Aunt Sophia and Hill the grocer and Mrs Silas and everyone down in the town said: "Oh no, come on Tobias. You're not going to lead us up the garden path this time!" And no one ran home to fetch an umbrella, and the washing was left hanging outside. The ladies walked about wearing their finest straw bonnets, and Mrs Silas stayed out in the market place selling fruit and berries and vegetables.

That afternoon down came the rain, splashing in the streets. Everyone who was out and about got thoroughly soaked, inside and out. Aunt Sophia's straw bonnet drooped down over her ears—Mrs Silas's berries starting running all over the square like syrup and juice, and the washing got so wet it had to be wrung out once again.

Everyone looked at one another in astonishment. "How peculiar," they said, "this time he *wasn't* kidding, but we were fooled just the same! Oh well."

Old Tobias has a young friend. His name is Remo. And young Remo and his dog, whose name is Bobby, often sit with Tobias up in the tower house looking at the clouds and gazing through the telescope at the stars.

"Can you see that star over there?" said Tobias one dark evening. "That's a wishing star. If it ever lies between the tips of the half moon you can wish almost anything you like."

"I'd wish that I could be as wise as you," said Remo.

"You're almost certain to be that anyway," considered Tobias.

"D'you think so?"

"Yes, I do. And when I get too old to sit here you can take my place in the tower and keep an eye on the weather in Cardamom Town."

"I don't think I'd be able to," said Remo, "I haven't got a beard."

"You'll get one all in good time," said old Tobias.

And he raised his telescope and looked out over the world while he sang his song about the weather in the east and the west and the north and the south:

THE WEATHER SONG

When it's close to harvest feast,
and the wind blows from the east,
then the rain comes pouring down
everywhere upon the town.
And in Cardamom high street
under cover people meet
if they do not have
galoshes on their feet.

9

When it's north from where they blow
and the winds bring only snow,
then the winter will arrive;
with some warm clothes you'll survive.
But if you are one of those
with no wish to wear warm clothes,
you'll be frozen blue
in all your toes and nose.

When the wind blows from the west
there is danger and unrest.
It could blow so hard one day
you might almost blow away.
And if your umbrella's thrown,
you could find you've upped and flown,
and away from Cardamom
you could be blown.

When the wind is in the south,
it brings laughter to my mouth.
For the weather forecast tells
there will be some frequent spells
of splendid sun, for summer's near,
and I call for all to hear:
"Hallo hallo, now watch these
sunny days appear!"

While Tobias sits up in his tower house keeping an eye on the weather, life jogs happily along down in Cardamom Town. People exchange friendly greetings with one another—"Good day," they say, "how are things this morning?" And in the middle of the street, donkeys plod by with panniers filled with oranges, dates and cardamom pods.

You won't find any motor cars here in Cardamom, but there is a tram, a single tram. It isn't big, and it doesn't go far. But the townsfolk are fond of their tram and take a short ride on it every day and often several times a day.

"Take your seats!" calls tram driver Puddleson, ringing the tram bell. Then the passengers hold tight, both grown ups and little ones. And off goes the tram. And everyone joins in singing tram driver Puddleson's tram song:

THE CARDAMOM TRAM

In the town of Cardamom our life is free from care.
Here there are no cars, but there's a tram for every fare.
I'm the tram conductor on the line called number one,
direction north to south is how we run.

> We start off every quarter hour,
> there's room to carry many more.
> And by the bridge is where we stop,
> we turn the tram round at the top.
> And if you want to ride straight back,
> just climb the stair beside the door,
> for you can ride the upper deck,
> and see the sights when there's no shower.
> Now all are seated we'll depart
> and now our tram can make a start.

11

The ticket for the journey here is absolutely free,
and passengers get little cakes for breakfast and for tea,
for Puddleson who drives the tram is such a friendly man,
who likes us all to be like him who can.

We drive with music and full song,
although our journey is not long.
But then we like to ride our line,
and as we go we sing and rhyme.
And if you please, just choose a cake,
there's cake for everyone to share.
And if the ride back home you make,
there's still some cake and more to spare.
Our journey takes one minute flat,
we ride until the stop we're at.

CHAPTER TWO—ABOUT THE THREE ROBBERS
CASPER AND JESPER AND JONATHAN

On a remote plain beyond Cardamom Town stands a tall and peculiar old house. That's where Casper and Jesper and Jonathan live. Casper is the eldest, Jesper the most handsome, and Jonathan the greediest, when it comes to food. The three of them are robbers, but they're not quite as bad as many other robbers, and they spend most of their time at home in their house.

13

For a sort of house pet, useful as well as cuddly, the robbers keep a lion. All things considered, he's a friendly sort of lion, and doesn't get into too many scrapes. Once he gobbled up Jesper's big toe—but, as Jonathan said, it didn't matter that much because when Jesper had his boots on, nobody noticed.

"Nevertheless, he's not like a lion ought to be," said Jesper.

"I only want to tell you," said Casper, "that a lion is the most useful pet we could have!"

"I know that perfectly well," said Jesper, "but it's not very pleasant to be eaten up, even if it is only a tiny morsel."

"Well, that was unfortunate, the lion probably just happened to be particularly hungry that day," said Jonathan. And Jonathan certainly knew the meaning of that—being hungry, that is.

"Our lion is very useful to us," said Casper. "Before, the house was full of rats and mice, but since we've had the lion—what then? No mice—no rats."

"I know that perfectly well, too," said Jesper.

"And remember this," said Casper, "that lion's the best guard we could have. Neither the Police Inspector nor anyone else

14

would dare to come here and arrest us as long as the lion's in the house."

"That's right, Jesper," said Jonathan.

"Yes, yes, yes," said Jesper, "but if I want to say how distasteful it is to be eaten, I must be allowed to say it!"

While they were wrangling like this they could hear the lion pacing back and forth in the bedroom, growling. The three robbers listened—and looked at one another.

"Now the lion's angry," said Jesper.

"He must be hungry," said Jonathan.

"Let him have the leftover sausages," said Casper.

"There don't seem to be any sausages left over," said Jesper. "Jonathan has eaten them all."

"That's a fact, that," said Jonathan.

"So let him have a piece of the ham in the bag we hung up in the roof rafters," said Casper.

"There doesn't seem to be any ham in the bag we hung up in the roof rafters," said Jesper.

"Isn't *that* there either?" asked Casper.

"Jonathan's eaten that, too?"

"Have you eaten that, as well?" asked Casper, who was beginning to get annoyed.

"It's just possible, that," said Jonathan—"you know how it is when you're hungry."

"Does that mean we haven't any meat left in the house?" asked Casper.

"Yes, that's what it means."

"Well, well," said Casper, "then there's nothing for it except to go robbing tonight!"

"That's a good idea for a whole lot of reasons," said Jonathan. "We need a little of everything—in fact."

"We'll set out as soon as it's dark," said Casper.

"Soon as it's dark," said Jesper.

"With buckets and bags," said Casper.

"With buckets and bags," said Jonathan.

And as soon as it was night and darkness had fallen, the three robbers locked the door of the robbers' house, and set off to rob the town.

ROBBERS' SONG

We sneak on tiptoe as we go
so stealthily to steal-o.
We take just what we need and know
where we can find a meal-o.
Now darkness lies upon the town,
asleep beneath its eiderdown.
We're off with our bag and our bucket and pan,
both Casper and Jesper and Jonathan.
    (Yes, that's what we do.)

The baker shop is where we stop,
we shan't pinch much from there though,
just bread and cake and soda pop
enough for us to share-o.
It's true that sometimes Jonathan
will grab himself a gingerman.
But then we make do just as best as we can,
both Casper and Jesper and Jonathan.
    (CASPER: Yes, Jonathan, he always
    has to have something to bite into.)

The butcher smokes a hock of ham
and cervelat and bacon;
loin of pork and rack of lamb,
to feed the lion, we've taken.
A rib of beef for roasting rare,
and sausages are spicy fare.
But then we make do just as best as we can,
both Casper and Jesper and Jonathan.
    (JONATHAN: Yes, we do that. But one
    needs a little something to live.)

And when it's cold we have to wear
some clothes to warm the body.
A winter coat against the air
which should not be too shoddy.
And socks and shirts and hats on top,
we know of just the very shop.
But then we make do just as best as we can,
both Casper and Jesper and Jonathan.
    (JESPER: In fact, I really could
    do with a new scarf.)

And when we're done with filling sacks
and buckets full of goods-o,
we heave them high upon our backs
and stagger through the woods-o.
And when we're home we eat the food
to satisfy our hungry mood.
But then we make do just as best as we can,
both Casper and Jesper and Jonathan.
    (Yes, that's what we do!)

It was the middle of the night and the town was in darkness when Casper and Jesper and Jonathan arrived at the pork butcher's. The pork butcher slept, and Police Inspector Bastian slept—and I think everyone else slept too, for no one was about in the streets.

"We have to be absolutely silent so we don't wake the pork butcher," said Casper. "We musn't make a sound," said Jonathan. And Jesper took out all his keys and found the one that fitted exactly the door of the pork butcher's. Then cautiously they crept in—the three of them.

Once inside, they found a huge store of best cuts of meat! Oy

oy oy! There were sausages and steaks and hams and joints. And the robbers crammed a little of everything into their buckets and bags. Then they carefully locked the door, and set off for the robbers' house, hungry and happy.

And now you're wondering what the pork butcher will say when he arrives at his shop the next morning to discover the robbers have been there during the night robbing him. We'll hear about that in the next chapter.

CHAPTER THREE—THE PORK BUTCHER
IS ANGRY AND POLICE INSPECTOR BASTIAN
IS UPSET—AND SILAS CAN'T GET HIS
DONKEY TO GO

The next day the pork butcher was furious when he arrived at his shop to discover the robbers had been there during the night and robbed him of joints and hams and steaks, as well as sausages. Even though he's usually a peaceable sort of fellow, he slammed his fist down onto the counter and fumed: "Now I'm going straight to Police Inspector Bastian to report this, and then he'll have to set about arresting the robbers!"

He left at once, and over by Sophia's yard he met Police Inspector Bastian just coming away merrily humming his little song.

"Superintendent!" shouted the pork butcher. "This won't do any longer!"

"No, it won't, at that," said Bastian. "And what is it, by the way, that won't do any longer?"

"The robbers have been in my shop last night and robbed me!"

"No, but that's shocking," said Bastian.

"It's a disgrace!" said the pork butcher.

"Yes, it is," said Bastian. "Have they stolen something, as well?"

"They've stolen four hams, two joints of beef as well as steaks and sausages!"

Bastian shook his head dejectedly. "That is bad news on a fine day like this," he said.

"Something's got to be done," said the pork butcher.

"It must, at that," said Bastian. "I shall note it down in my book."

"The robbers have to be arrested!" said the pork butcher. "At once!"

"Yes, yes," said Bastian. "All in good time. The first thing is to write it down, and then give the matter careful consideration."

"The robbers should have been arrested ages ago!" said the pork butcher, who by now was so angry as to be almost impudent.

Police Inspector Bastian frowned at him. "Listen here, my dear pork butcher! Have *you* ever arrested folk who keep a lion?"

"No," said the pork butcher. "But I'm *not* a Police Inspector."

"I won't be a Police Inspector either—by the time the lion has eaten me up," said Bastian.

"My apologies, Mr Bastian," said the pork butcher, "I hadn't thought of that."

"What's more, it's also a very awkward day on which to arrest anyone," said Bastian. "You must, I'm sure, be aware that it's Cardamom Day tomorrow, and I have a great deal to think about. After all, we're holding the fête in the town square and gardens with the Town Orchestra, and there's singing and dancing, and much more."

"Yes, yes, I know all about that. But I just wanted it put down," said the pork butcher.

"I shall consider the matter immediately and at once," said Police Inspector Bastian. "I shall think about it all while I'm proceeding down the street."

Then each bowed politely to the other and went on his way.

But up on the balcony of her house, Miss Aunt Sophia had heard the whole conversation between Police Inspector Bastian and the pork butcher. And she's absolutely appalled.

AUNT SOPHIA'S SONG

O fiddlesticks o fiddlesticks,
I'm angry and I'll frown!
It's stuff and nonsense everywhere
in Cardamom our town!
If only people were like me—
it would be very good.
But no one is at all like me—
they don't do what they should.
    Huff!

Now see Inspector Bastian
who's simply mild and kind,
to do his job that's not enough
for him to have in mind!
A real policeman has to be
a strict and angry man,
and go about arresting folk
as often as he can.
　　Yes!

And our Inspector falls asleep
and never hears a sound
when robbers go to work at night
and lurk and slink around.
But if they think they're coming here,
they've got another thought,
I shall be sitting here in wait—
and I shall see them caught!
　　Yes!

Police Inspector Bastian walked down the street thinking about the robbers and the pork butcher's. But he didn't find the time to think for long, because down in the square a crowd of people were standing in a circle round something or other.

"What's going on here?" enquired Bastian.

"It's Silas's donkey. It won't go," explained Patterson the barber.

"Yes, have you ever seen the like," said Silas, "you'd think this donkey was completely stubborn. It won't budge an inch!"

"You're holding up the traffic in the street, my good Silas," said Police Inspector Bastian.

23

"All right, I know that," said Silas. "But what can I do if the donkey *will* not go?"

"Is it a heavy load you've got there?" asked Bastian.

"No, not at all, quite the opposite. It's just empty potato sacks."

"Well, well—we must help to push the animal," said Bastian. "Come on everyone," he called.

And so everyone helped—barber Patterson and Hill the grocer, and the cobbler and tram driver Puddleson. Some *pulled* the donkey, and some *pushed*. "Giddy up!" they said. And then— then the donkey stood just as still on the same spot.

"This is peculiar," said Police Inspector Bastian scratching his neck.

"Yes, but that's just like the animal," said Silas. "It'll be standing here all today and tomorrow too if it doesn't suddenly change its mind."

Bastian was crestfallen and shook his head. "Today is a most unfortunate day for the donkey to be standing still," he said. "Surely you know what day it is tomorrow, Silas, and I have a great deal to think about."

"Yes," said Silas, "it's just as bad as it *can* be!"

"Here comes old Tobias!" said barber Patterson. "Perhaps *he* can find a solution."

"Yes, he's a wise man," said grocer Hill.

And Silas bowed and said: "Excuse us, Mr Tobias. We could do with your best advice. *Here we are at a standstill.* That's to say: the donkey's at a standstill. It won't move itself. And there's our tram at a standstill, and it can't get past. And *there's* Police Inspector Bastian at a standstill. *What shall I do?*"

"H'm," said Tobias, pausing for thought. "Perhaps you'd unhitch the cart, then we'll see," he said.

"That—that won't help," said Silas. But he did as old Tobias suggested.

"And now, Silas, now push the cart up alongside the donkey—here." So Silas did.

"Now," said Tobias, "everyone get a good grip on the animal, and then we'll lift the donkey up into the cart. One—two—three—hup!"

And the donkey was lifted up into the empty cart, and there it stood looking around in surprise.

"That's *that*," said Tobias. "And now, Silas, now you can just get in here and hold the shafts, and then you can drive home with your donkey."

Silas didn't feel that was right, but he did as Tobias commanded. He grasped both shafts and began to pull. And the donkey stood up in the cart and enjoyed being driven instead of having to pull. "Ha ha ha," it went, just as donkeys usually do.

The others laughed: "Oh, that Tobias, he's got the answer to almost everything," they said. But Silas was a little surly: "*That's the way to spoil the animal!*" he said.

But at least the street was clear again, and the tram was able to continue on its usual route through the town. And tram driver Puddleson and the passengers could sing their happy song.

"Yes, yes," said barber Patterson, "I'd better be off home. We've a rehearsal for the Town Orchestra due to start about now, in preparation for tomorrow's fête."

Back home, his three good friends were waiting. They were grocer Hill who played the horn, drummer Parker, and Anderson, the swimming instructor and music teacher, who played flute. They all had their instruments.

"Together now, let's go," said barber Patterson. "One, two, three!" Then they rehearsed all the tunes they planned to play at the Cardamom fête the following day.

CHAPTER FOUR—IT'S CARDAMOM DAY BUT AUNT SOPHIA WON'T ALLOW LITTLE CAMOMILLA TO GO TO THE FÊTE

So the day came for the great summer fête in Cardamom Town. It began quite early in the morning with the Cardamom Town Orchestra setting up in the square and striking up the Cardamom March. And the musicians were grocer Hill on horn, drummer Parker, swimming instructor and music teacher Anderson on flute, and barber Patterson on clarinet. And the four of them wore white caps—and flowers in their buttonholes.

The sun shone and the houses were decked with flowers and bunting in the splendid summer weather. The children had the day off from school, and the grown ups were free from work too. And grown ups and little ones wore their Sunday best, even though it was a Tuesday.

The whole town was on its way to the great Cardamom fête in the town square and gardens. Well, not quite the whole town. Little Camomilla wasn't going. Aunt Sophia wouldn't allow her to go. Camomilla was very upset, because she wanted to go to the fête so much. But there was nothing to be done; whatever Aunt Sophia said, that's how it had to be. So Camomilla sat at her piano, instead, and practised her music lesson, because it comforted her to play a little.

As she sat playing a little waltz, her best friend Tommy came along. He was riding his donkey, whose name is Pontius. Tommy stopped beside the window and listened to the music and thought it sounded very pretty indeed.

CAMOMILLA PLAYS

Hear me in my forte
play my pianoforte—
one and two and three and
one and two and three.
I am counting right and
reading notes by sight and—
one and two and three and
one and two and three.

I play exercises,
with some small surprises—
one and two and three and
one and two and three—
little waltz with couplets
called "Four Pocket Trumpets"—
one and two and three and
one and two and three.

If I always listen,
never miss a lesson—
one and two and three and
one and two and three—
I shall learn so many
pieces sad and sunny.
Only wait till I am big
and you will see.
One and two and three.

"Hallo Camomilla," called Tommy. At which, Camomilla came out onto the balcony. "How prettily you play," he said.

"Do you think so?" said Camomilla, who was overjoyed to hear him say that.

"My Dad plays well, too," said Tommy. "He plays the horn."

"That's a lovely instrument, too," said Camomilla.

"The Town Orchestra's playing at the fête today. You should come and hear him."

"Oh yes, but I'm not going there," said Camomilla.

"Why ever not?" puzzled Tommy.

"Aunt Sophia says that fêtes and amusements aren't suitable for little girls. So I have to stay at home, and Aunt Sophia, too."

29

"That's a shame," said Tommy sadly, "because if you could come you could have a ride on Pontius."

"Yes, that is a great shame."

"But listen, Camomilla! Can't you slip out without Aunt Sophia noticing, then I could help you get down from the balcony."

"No, I wouldn't dare to," said Camomilla, "Aunt Sophia is so . . ."

"No, no. We'll have to find another way." Tommy thought for a moment, but it wasn't all that easy to find another way. "Camomilla," he said, "I'll go and talk to old Tobias. He's sure to have some good advice."

"Do you think so?"

"Yes, you bet.—I'll be back soon."

Tommy mounted Pontius and rode off to the square. And up in his tower house old Tobias was peering through his telescope at the weather.

"Hallo Tobias!" shouted Tommy.

Old Tobias took the telescope away from his eye and looked down at Tommy and Pontius. "Oh, it's you, Tommy?"

"Yes," said Tommy. "I have to talk to you about something. Aunt Sophia won't allow little Camomilla to go to the fête. Isn't that a shame?"

"Yes, a shame indeed," said Tobias.

"Aunt Sophia says that fêtes and amusements aren't suitable for little girls!"

"Oh dear, that Aunt Sophia. She's not an easy one. But look here, Tommy. We must see what we can do to help little Camomilla."

"That's what we have to do," said Tommy.

Tobias thought for a moment. "I think I've got it," he said. "We must find someone to get Aunt Sophia to go to the fête, because if

30

Aunt Sophia goes to the fête, then little Camomilla can't be left at home on her own, and so Camomilla will have to come too."

"That's pretty smart," said Tommy.

"Smart it is," said Tobias, "but difficult. For who can you think of who might be brave enough to invite Miss Sophia?"

"No, there can't be many," said Tommy.

"No, there can't be," pondered Tobias. "The thing to do is to find the right person."

"Yes," said Tommy, "*that's* the thing to do."

"Perhaps—I should try myself," proposed Tobias.

"Yes, *that* would definitely be the right person," said Tommy.

"Give me a moment to get ready," said Tobias, "I just have to spruce myself up a little and put a hat on my head."

And three minutes later old Tobias and Pontius and Tommy were off to Aunt Sophia's house.

"It might be best if you and your donkey go a little further down the street and wait there," said Tobias.

"Yes," agreed Tommy, "it might be best if she doesn't see there are several of us."

Tobias strode forward and knocked firmly but gently on the door. Knock, knock!

"Who is it?" enquired a voice from inside.

"Ah, Miss Aunt Sophia, it's only me."

Aunt Sophia opened up. "So, is it you?" she said.

"Yes, it's me," answered Tobias. "I've come to invite you to the Cardamom fête. Yes, you know . . ."

"No, thank you, I'm not off to any Cardamom fête. And furthermore I cannot. I have to stay at home to look after little Camomilla."

"Ah, but my dear Miss Sophia—you can just as well bring little Camomilla with you."

"No, I most certainly cannot. She's far too small for fêtes and amusements."

"Oh—she's big enough," said Tobias. "It's meant to be a family fête, for children, too, and, amongst other things, I shall be singing a song, for I've promised Police Inspector Bastian I would."

"Is that so, indeed?"

"Yes, it's true," said Tobias smiling proudly.

Aunt Sophia thought for a moment. Then she said: "Very well—I shall come along."

"That's splendid," said Tobias, overwhelmed.

"We shall see," answered Aunt Sophia. She turned and called into the house: "Camomilla! You'll have to come to the fête!"

"Hurrah!" shouted Camomilla.

"Hush, child, stop with the hurrahs! Go upstairs and wash.—Mr Tobias," she said, "We'll be with you in a moment." And Miss Sophia went into the house and closed the door after her. Old Tobias waited outside smiling proudly. He gave a discreet thumbs up to Tommy and Pontius who were peeping out from behind the corner of a house.

A quarter of an hour later Aunt Sophia and little Camomilla stepped out of the door—all dressed up.

"Good day to you, little Camomilla," said Tobias.

33

"Good day, Tobias," said Camomilla.

And who should they meet round the corner but Tommy and Pontius.

"Well I never—here's Tommy, too," said Tobias. "Are you off to the fête as well, then?"

"That's exactly where I'm going," answered Tommy.

"But you could just as well come along with us," said Tobias. "Don't you think so, Miss Sophia?"

"Certainly," answered Sophia.

"If Camomilla wishes, she's very welcome to ride on Pontius," said Tommy.

"Oh, yes, I'd love to," said Camomilla beaming with pleasure. Old Tobias lifted her up onto the donkey's back and Tommy walked along by the side, leading the donkey.

"Camomilla is now permitted to do everything, it seems," said Aunt Sophia.

And that's how it was that the four of them went to the fête, one riding and three walking.

CHAPTER FIVE—ABOUT THE PERFORMANCE IN THE TOWN SQUARE—AND THE GARDEN FÊTE

The fête was already under way in the square. There were musicians and people enjoying themselves. And first and foremost there was Police Inspector Bastian.

"Good day to you, Tobias," he said, "many thanks for the fine weather, by the way! And good day to you, Miss Sophia. How splendid you could come too. Please be good enough to find a seat, and do excuse me, I have so much to think about." And Bastian scuttled off.

"Huff, what a fusspot!" exclaimed Aunt Sophia.

Between the palm tree and the tower house, tram driver Puddleson had draped a beautiful stage curtain, and erected a small

35

stage where the performance was going to take place. As the hands of the clock approached five, people took their places on the benches, for the show was about to begin. Tobias and Aunt Sophia and Tommy and little Camomilla found seats in the front row, while Pontius had to sit quietly on the ground beside them.

"Yes, these are very good seats," remarked old Tobias. And little by little Aunt Sophia's mood changed for the better.

Police Inspector Bastian walked to the front of the stage, ringing a large bell, to announce the programme they were about to see and hear. "Dear assembled company," he said, "welcome to our great family show. To open our performance the Town Orchestra will play the Cardamom Song, and you're all requested to join in and sing, and enjoy yourselves. One—two—three!"

The orchestra began to play, and grown ups and little ones joined in and sang, for this was a song they all knew:

THE CARDAMOM SONG

Here our life in Cardamom has problems far and few.
Everyone is happy, for we take things as we do.
The baker bakes a pastry, and the cobbler mends a shoe.
And everyone has dinner when it's two.

Oh Cardamom is where we stay,
we never want to go away.
Police Inspector Bastian
is top to toe the world's best man.
And we have trumpet, fife and drummer
if you'd like to join the dance,
and Cardamom Town Fête Orchestra
plays non stop without a glance.
Hurrah hurrah we sing our cheers,
and we'll live here a hundred years.

"And now," said Police Inspector Bastian, "our dear friend Tobias will sing his song about the weather in the east and west and north and south. A big hand for Tobias!"

Old Tobias came forward onto the stage, bowed to the audience, raised his telescope, and sang about the weather. And everyone applauded their favourite weather forecaster.

"A thousand thanks," said Bastian, "that was a cheerful song. And now, dear friends," he said, "we've an exceptional and unique turn. It's 'The Talking Camel'!—Yes, it's a very rare camel that can talk, and this one is rarer still, this camel also sings. Here he comes—'The Talking Camel'!"

The curtain opened to reveal the camel. He looked around in surprise, nodded his head and began to sing:

With sacks of cinnamon and peppa'
between south and north I walk,
and I am known in every township
as the camel that can talk.
And how to talk I learnt when I was little
from a dromedar'—
who said he'd learnt it from his ma,
who said she'd learnt it from her pa.

While everyone clapped and cheered the camel, Police Inspector Bastian went over to the bench where old Tobias and Aunt Sophia and Tommy and little Camomilla were sitting. Bastian was a little nervous, to say the least:

"Dear Miss Sophia," he said, "a very unfortunate thing has just occurred. Our singer, who was about to sing for us, is so hoarse she can't reach a single note. Wouldn't you sing a little song in her place?"

"No," said Aunt Sophia.

"Oh, won't you, kind Miss Sophia? It would be such a treat!"

Aunt Sophia raised her head. "I have only *one* song," she said, "and it is *not* suitable for today."

"Of course it is," said Police Inspector Bastian, "all songs are suitable for today. Please join in, if you'd be so kind!"

"It would be such a great treat," said old Tobias.

"Well," she said, "I'll sing then—the song is *not* suitable for today, as you'll find out soon enough."

"A thousand thanks," said Police Inspector Bastian. And he jumped excitedly up onto the stage and rang his clapper bell:

"And now, dear friends," he said, "I've been lucky enough to persuade Aunt Sophia to sing a song for us. She herself says the song isn't suitable for today—but I'm sure it is. A big hand for Miss Sophia!"

Aunt Sophia stepped up onto the stage, straightened her hat a little and then began to sing:

AUNT SOPHIA'S ANGRY SONG

O fiddlesticks o fiddlesticks, I'm angry and I'll frown!
It's stuff and nonsense everywhere in Cardamom our town.
If only people were like me—it would be very good.
But no one is at all like me—they don't do what they should.
  Huff!

39

Now see Inspector Bastian who's simply mild and kind,
to do his job that's not enough for him to have in mind!
A real policeman has to be a strict and angry man,
and go about arresting folk as often as he can.
    Yes!

And tram conductor Puddleson—he sings to make us glad,
but if you drive a tram that way it's really very bad.
He shouldn't sing, he shouldn't laugh, he shouldn't think
   in rhyme.
He should only drive his tram at such a serious time.
    Yes!

And boys are free to misbehave and never get the stick,
and cake and cream is all they eat, enough to make them sick.
If they were mine—I wouldn't let them go without a wash—
not one would get a sweet from me—I've never heard such tosh!
    No!

And our Inspector falls asleep, and never hears a sound,
when robbers go to work at night and lurk and slink around.
But if they think they're coming here, they've got another
   thought,
I shall be sitting here in wait—and I shall see them caught!
    Yes!

"That was the song!" said Aunt Sophia, who quickly got down and sat back in her place. There was much merriment, and almost everyone applauded, including Police Inspector Bastian, though a bit hesitantly.

"Very many thanks," he said, "that,—that was a—a—an *entertaining* song. Many thanks!" And then he rang the bell again.

"The next number is also exceptional and unique," he said. "It's the Cardamom Canine Chorus, consisting of Hannibal,

Bobby and barber Patterson's dog. They're going to sing that old favourite about the Sleeping Beauty who slept for a hundred years. And Bobby and his friends will sing it in their own canine language!"

Bobby and Hannibal and barber Patterson's dog lined themselves up in a neat row, and then the song began. Barber Patterson's poodle, who was the smallest of the dogs, barked the highest notes, while Bobby, an enormous guard dog, barked the lowest notes. Everything went splendidly until they were almost halfway through the song. Then, suddenly, the most almighty pandemonium broke out. All three dogs leapt, barking, down from the stage and out across the square, and wouldn't come back before Bastian had rung his bell several times. The audience collapsed in laughter, but Bastian was a bit taken aback.

"I apologize for this slight hitch in the performance," he said. "A black cat darted in front of the stage, and the dogs forgot themselves. But now Mrs Silas has recovered her cat, and we'll try again from the beginning."

This time it went off well. The dogs sang the whole melody, and everyone applauded Bobby and Hannibal and barber Patterson's dog enthusiastically.

41

And so the performance in the square came to a close. "But the fête continues in the town gardens," announced Bastian, "where there's music and a merry-go-round and the wheel of fortune. And for those who wish there'll also be the opportunity to take a short ride on the talking camel."

In the gardens there was also Bandini with his elephant. The elephant's name is Grosso and he's very big. There were seats on top of the elephant's back. And kind old Tobias bought three elephant tickets so that Aunt Sophia, Tommy and little Camomilla were able to enjoy a ride on Grosso, while Pontius stayed tethered to a tree for ever so long.

CHAPTER SIX—ABOUT THREE WHO DIDN'T GO TO THE FÊTE

Everything went swimmingly in the town gardens. But there were a few who didn't get to join in the festivities—they were the robbers Casper and Jesper and Jonathan who had clambered up into a tree where no one could discover them. From there, they could see the merry-go-round and the elephant and the talking camel and a little of everything.

"It looks like great fun down in the gardens," said Jonathan.

"We're having fun too," said Casper.

"Not *such* fun," said Jesper. He'd just caught sight of little Camomilla riding the talking camel. "They're lucky, the ones who get to ride on that," he said.

"It would be fun to have a go once," said Jonathan.

43

Jesper thought so too, and in his eagerness he nearly fell out of the tree. "Hey, you," he said, "d'you know what we could do? We could go along tonight when the fête's over, and then we could *carry off the camel!*"

"Hold your horses," said Casper. "We haven't got much use for a camel!"

"Haven't we—well, we have at that."

"What on earth for?" queried Casper.

"Well, for example, when we go out robbing we could ride there and back, and then we wouldn't have to carry those heavy sacks all the way home."

"Yes, and then we could bring back a lot more each time," said Jonathan.

"We can't have a camel with us when we're out robbing, really!" said Casper, irritated.

"And, why not?"

"Just because we *can't*. What do you think would happen when we want to get the camel in and out of the pork butcher's doors?"

"That's true, Jesper," said Jonathan.

"And how do you think we'd get it *up* the stairs and *down* the stairs?" asked Casper.

"No, no, so we won't make off with the camel," said Jesper, offended.

They sat in silence for a moment looking into the gardens. But then Jesper said: "All things considered, it's a great pity we're never able to join in the fête and such."

"Yes, it's a shame," said Jonathan, "because they're bound to be getting something good to eat down there!"

"Everything's just fine for us just as it is," said Casper.

"There's another thing I think's a shame too," said Jonathan, "*we* never get to ride on the tram."

"That's not much fun, either," said Casper.

"It certainly is fun," insisted Jonathan.

At that, Jesper hit on a scheme: "Jonathan," he said, "I've a great idea."

"What?" asked Jonathan. "Come on, out with it!"

"Well," said Jesper. "We're sitting here. The tram driver's down in the gardens. And the tram's over in the square—all on its own."

"Aha, Jesper. I see what you're getting at."

"We'll—steal—we'll go joy riding on the tram!"

"Yes, lads. That's exactly what we'll do," said Jonathan gleefully.

"They climbed down carefully from the tree and slipped over to the tram. But Casper was a bit apprehensive. "D'you think we'll be able to start it?" he asked.

"Nothing to it," said Jesper, "we just *crank* a bit here and *ring* a bit there—then it'll go."

And they did, and it went.

"That was fun," said Jesper and Jonathan. And Casper was pretty keen now, too, because he was standing in the front, steering. "It must be exciting to be the tram driver," he said.

The tramlines didn't go further than the town gate, so the tram had to stop there. But the robbers were in a jolly mood after the excitement of their tram ride. And inside the tram Jesper and Jonathan had found a whole crateful of delicious cakes.

"We'll take them home to the robbers' house," said Jonathan. Jesper and Jonathan carried the crate between them, and the three of them made their way home, happy and content. Now they too were able to celebrate Cardamom Day.

A little later that evening, barber Patterson and tram driver Puddleson returned to the square. They were in a jolly mood.

"Yes, things are going well, tram driver Puddleson," said barber Patterson.

"Indeed, they are," replied tram driver Puddleson. "I've just had a little ride on the merry-go-round and that was pretty . . . but Patter—son!" he suddenly cried out in alarm, "what's happened to the tram?"

"The tram?" echoed barber Patterson.

"Yes, the tram," said Puddleson, pointing across to the tram stop. "I left the tram right there, but it *isn't* there. Police Inspector!" he shouted, "the tram's been stolen!"

And Police Inspector Bastian came running out of the town gardens. He shook his head. "No, *that* can't be possible!" he said.

"Yes, it is," said Puddleson. "I left the tram right *there*, and you can see for yourself, it's not there."

"This is mysterious," said Bastian, examining the area closely.

"Yes, it is," said barber Patterson.

Bastian was a bit annoyed. "It's a most unfortunate day for the tram to disappear," he said. "Well, well, I'll note it down in my book."—Suddenly, a thought occurred to him. "Tram driver," he

asked, "can the tram go even where there aren't any tramlines?"

"No, Police Inspector, quite impossible," said tram driver Puddleson.

"Then the tram has to be somewhere or other between here and the town gate, surely?"

"Yes, it has to be," said Puddleson.

"Then we're bound to find it again," said Police Inspector Bastian. "Follow me—in the name of the law!"

They found the tram at the town gate, quite safe and sound. It was Police Inspector Bastian who spotted it first. "There's the tram!" he exclaimed proudly.

"We've found it," said barber Patterson.

"Quite safe and sound," said tram driver Puddleson. "But the crate of cakes has disappeared."

"Yes, but all things considered, that's not a great calamity, now," suggested Bastian. "Everyone's eaten so much cake and confectionery today they can do without cake tomorrow."

Tram driver Puddleson rang the tram bell. "Take your seats!" he called. And Bastian and barber Patterson sat down, and soon the tram was back in the square.

Everyone in the square was happy to see the tram back where it belonged and clapped their hands. "Hurrah for the tram!" cried grown ups and little ones, "and hurrah for tram driver Puddleson and Inspector Bastian!"

Bastian himself was absolutely delighted. "And now let the Cardamom fête resume!" he said. And it did. And everyone joined in and sang as the Town Orchestra struck up the Cardamom Song once again.

CARDAMOM SONG

In the town of Cardamom our life is free from care.
Here there are no cars, but there's a tram for every fare.
I'm the tram conductor on the line called number one,
direction north to south is how we run.

Oh Cardamom is where we stay,
we never want to go away.
Police Inspector Bastian
is top to toe the world's best man.
And we have trumpet, fife and drummer,
if you'd like to join the dance,
and Cardamom Town Fête Orchestra
plays non stop without a glance.
Hurrah hurrah we sing our cheers,
and we'll live here a hundred years.

CHAPTER SEVEN—A NIGHT OF SUSPENSE AT THE PORK BUTCHER'S

Cardamom Day was over. The tram that was stolen was found again, and Police Inspector Bastian's days were quiet and uneventful. But the baker and the pork butcher and grocer Hill never felt completely at ease. So they didn't sleep at night as soundly as other townsfolk. And one dark night the pork butcher woke up, thinking he heard suspicious noises from his shop below.

"It's definitely the robbers here again," he said to his wife. He leapt out of bed and grabbed his trousers. "Now I'll catch them, at last," he said.

"You won't manage it on your own," said his wife, "because there's sure to be three of them."

"I'll have the baker and Police Inspector Bastian with me, don't you worry," said the pork butcher. He crept down the stairs and out the door and across to the house on the corner where the baker lived.

"Baker, wake up!" he called.

"Is something the matter?" asked the baker.

"The robbers have come robbing!"

"Me oh my," said the baker and he was out of bed like a shot, too, groping for his trousers. "Where are the robbers?" he asked.

"In my shop," said the pork butcher, "and now we'll catch the three of them, at last."

"Then we need Police Inspector Bastian with us," said the baker.

"We certainly do," said the pork butcher.

So off they went to the police station and woke up the Police Inspector.

"Now the robbers have come robbing again," said the pork butcher.

"That can't be possible," said Bastian who wasn't wide awake yet.

"Oh yes it is, and now we'll capture them, at last."

"Yes, we must," said Bastian. He buttoned up his trousers and smart jacket. "Be careful," said Mrs Bastian.

"Yes, we will," Bastian reassured her. And the three of them slipped over to the pork butcher's to catch the robbers.

ROBBER CATCHING SONG

We must be so silent,
the silence must not wake,
so we can catch the robber rogues
and punish their mistake.
They're not the kindest people!
We want a quick arrest.
For each is just a rascal
like every robber pest.

They've taken all my sausage
and cervelat and ham
and roasting beef and chicken stock
and venison and lamb.
I'm sick and tired of trouble,
we want a quick arrest!
For each is just a rascal
like every robber pest.

From me, and I'm the baker,
they've taken Danish pastry,
current buns with icing on
and fancy loaves and pasty.
No more cake and crumble,
we want a quick arrest!
For each is just a rascal
like every robber pest.

Outside the pork butcher's they stopped to listen, and heard some suspicious sounds coming from inside.

"We have to be careful," said Police Inspector Bastian, "because they might have the lion with them."

"There's a window open," said the baker.

"That's odd," said the pork butcher.

"That's probably where the robbers entered," concluded Bastian.

And so they set about planning how to capture the robbers. The baker was to keep watch outside the back door so no one could get out that way. "And pork butcher, you crawl in through that window and see no one comes out through there. Meanwhile, I'll unlock the door to the shop—and then we'll corner them from three directions at once. Any questions?"

51

"Understood," said the pork butcher and he crept over to the window.

Police Inspector Bastian was handed the keys to the front door, unlocked it cautiously—took a deep breath—flung open the door, and then shouted at the top of his voice: "You're arrested—in the name of the law!"

The light was dim inside the shop. They heard a thud on the floor and caught sight of someone or something scurrying behind the counter.

"Come out of there!" shouted Bastian. "We've seen you!"

For a moment it was quiet and no one appeared. But then up popped a tousled head. And what a surprise Police Inspector Bastian had—and the pork butcher too. For this was no *great* robber. It was Bobby—little Remo's dog.

"So, then. You're the robber," said Bastian.

"What a shame," said the pork butcher.

"What's a shame?" asked Bastian.

"That it wasn't the three robbers, of course. If it had been, we'd have caught them."

"Indeed, we would," said Bastian.

"Well," said the pork butcher, "you'll have to arrest the dog instead."

"Do you think so?" asked Bastian.

"Absolutely!" said the pork butcher. "I insist. He's certainly eaten both steaks and sausages. I can see he has, his stomach's so distended."

And Bobby was arrested in the name of the law. Police Inspector Bastian attached a leash to Bobby's collar and led him away.

Outside the shop, the baker was keeping watch. "Didn't you capture the robbers?" he asked in astonishment.

"This is the robber," retorted Bastian. And off he went to the police station with Bobby.

Next morning a small boy stood outside the police station. It was Remo. He knocked on the door and Police Inspector Bastian called, "Come in!" And Remo went in.

"So, it's you," said Bastian.

"My dog has gone," said Remo.

"Really," said Bastian.

"Yes," said Remo. "He's been gone all night."

"Your dog just got himself arrested," said Bastian. "He was out last night robbing the pork butcher of steaks and sausages."

"That can't have been Bobby," said Remo.

"Oh yes, it can," said Bastian.

"Where's Bobby now?" asked Remo.

"He's being held in custody. But he's comfortable enough," said Bastian.

Remo was led to the holding cell, where his dog lay asleep on a rug, exhausted but content after all he had eaten at the pork butcher's during the night. When he saw Remo, Bobby wagged his tail.

"Bad dog," said Remo. "Is it true you've robbed the pork butcher of steaks and sausages?"

Then Bobby hung his head in shame and looked down at the floor.

"Bobby says he'll never do it again," said Remo.

"Well, well. I'll let him off just this once," said Bastian. "And I do think the pork butcher ought to make sure his window's securely shut at night."

Remo got his dog back. And then he raced off with Bobby to visit old Tobias in the tower.

CHAPTER EIGHT—IN WHICH JONATHAN HITS ON A SCHEME—AND THE ROBBERS GO TO TOWN TO CARRY OFF AUNT SOPHIA

Following the day of their joy ride on the tram, Casper and Jesper and Jonathan spent a long period at home in their house. And everything in the house was just as it usually was. It was all one big mess, and every day the robbers bickered about who should do this and who should do that.

The mess piled up all over the place. None of them liked clearing up and none of them did it. None of them liked washing up and none of them did that either. And so everything lay in disorder here, there and everywhere, and no one knew why. Casper and Jesper and Jonathan scurried around one another looking for shirts and trousers and cups and plates:

THE ROBBERS LOOK

Where's my trousers gone? Where's my best shirt gone?
Where's the mouth organ then with only four notes in?
Where is Jesper's hat? Where is this and that?
Where's the brand new leather purse with very few notes in?
I can say I had it with me yesterday.

Where's my teacup gone? Where's my braces gone?
Where's the ladders and the holes in my old stocking toes?
Where is Casper's saw—and my hat of straw?
Where's the loop to hang my jersey, it no longer shows?
I can say I had it with me yesterday.

Where's the wicker bin with the peaches in?
Where's the marmalade and rusty old anchovy tin?
Where's the big broomstick? Where's the small toothpick?
Where's the khaki coloured stocking slippers' lace up string?
I can say I had it with me yesterday.

Where's the sack and can? Where's the pheasant flan?
Where is Casper? Where is Jesper? Where is Jonathan?
Where's the host and guest? Where's the east and west?
Where's the money box we stole from granny's treasure chest?
I can say I had it with me on the way.

"It's impossible to find anything in this house!" said Casper. "I've looked high and low but my socks *are* gone and *stay* gone!"

"It has to be the lion who's eaten them up," proposed Jonathan. "He's very fond of socks—you know."

That made Casper cross. "It's always the lion's fault," he said. "Whenever something goes wrong, blame the lion."

"All said and done, it was a mean trick for the lion to bite off one of my big toes that time," said Jesper. "It's a body blow—losing a toe."

"It was just because the lion was hungry that day," said Jonathan. "And that's not such a good thing—being hungry either. Come to think of it, aren't we going to have a bite to eat? It's almost dark and we haven't even had dinner!"

"And you know why, don't you? It's because no one will *make* any food," said Casper.

"I think Jonathan should do it," said Jesper, "because he never does a thing."

But then Jonathan replied: "What's the sense in being a robber at all if you still have to slave away all the time, anyway. And, as a matter of fact, it was me who made the goulash yesterday."

"Then Jesper can make the food," said Casper.

At that, Jesper took offense: "That's so unfair, because I eat less than both of you put together!"

Nevertheless Jesper went into the kitchen and started messing about with pots and pans. But then he changed his mind, threw the pan on the floor and stammered: "I'm—*not*—making—the food!"

"Well, well," said Casper, "then there won't *be* any food."

"What a pity," said Jonathan.

"It's always the same nonsense," said Casper. "No one wants to clear up, so no one *does*. No one wants to make the food, so no one does *that* either!—I'll tell you what we need: a woman about the house!"

"Ah, yes," said Jesper—"a really good housekeeper!"

"Then we can stop worrying about having to do everything ourselves," said Jonathan.

"That's exactly what we need," said Casper.

"But there can't be anyone who'd want to be here in the house with us," mused Jesper. And the three of them had to admit that.

Then Jonathan hit upon a scheme: "Perhaps we could *steal* someone," he said.

And they all became enthusiastic. Even the lion, who was lying in bed, raised his head and pricked up his ears.

"It has to be someone who's good at looking after pigs and lions," said Casper.

"And someone who's good at keeping the house in order," said Jesper.

"And who's a good cook," said Jonathan.

Casper smiled. "I think I know someone," he said slyly.

"Who's that?" asked Jesper. "Out with it," said Jonathan.

"Right, then," said Casper, "we're—going—to—carry—off—Miss—Aunt—Sophia, because she has to be good at making food and keeping house."

"What a brilliant idea!" agreed Jesper.

"But she's supposed to be a bit of an ogre," said Jonathan.

"Ogre!" exclaimed Casper. "Three big robbers like us aren't afraid of women folk, surely."

"There's something else I'm thinking about," said Jesper—"*how* are we going to carry her off?"

"That's easy enough," said Casper. "We can carry her off tonight. We'll steal into town and into the house where she lives and *then carry her off while she's asleep*!"

"What if she wakes?" said Jonathan.

"*She won't wake!*"

"Then it's settled," the three of them said, and got themselves ready for town.

"Shall we bring the lion along?" asked Jesper.

"Not the lion," said Casper, "it'll only make a noise. Put him in Jonathan's bed and shut the door properly. Have we got the keys?"

"Here are the keys!" said Jesper, jangling a big bunch of keys. Casper unhooked the lantern off the wall. "Everyone ready?" he asked. "Everyone ready," answered the others.

Then off they set for town. Casper went in front swinging the lantern, then Jesper with the key ring, and last of all Jonathan with a mouthful of sausage.

ROBBERS' SONG

We sneak on tiptoe as we go
so stealthily to steal-o.
A lady housemaid who we know
will make our daily meal-o.
And she will keep the whole house straight
and make our beds when we sleep late.
Yes, now we can think about many a plan,
both Casper and Jesper and Jonathan.
    "Yes, that'll be a new life, that!"

And she will tidy our affairs
and muck out in the lion's den.
Make mutton stew and syrup pears,
and bake cake in the oven.
And polish shoes for every male
and chop the wood and fetch the pail.
For now we will do just as little we can—
both Casper and Jesper and Jonathan.
    "Yes, that's what we'll do."

The town was dark and silent. Even Police Inspector Bastian slept. The robbers stole down the street.

"That's the house where she lives," said Casper.

Jesper selected the right key and the door was soon opened. Everyone listened.

"What sort of a noise is that?" asked Jonathan.

"That's just Miss Sophia snoring," whispered Jesper, and he crept into the house. The others waited outside.

Before long Jesper was back, laughing fit to burst: "Oh dear," he said, "Miss Sophia's asleep in the kitchen. She's—lying—in—a—hammock!"

61

"Oh, that's just great," said Casper, "then all we have to do is lift the hammock off its hooks and carry the whole shebang along, Sophia and all! And you, Jonathan, wait here!"

"Right, then. I'll wait," said Jonathan.

No sooner said than done. Jonathan stood watch outside with the lantern, while Casper and Jesper crept into the kitchen, carefully unhitched the hammock, and between them carried it out into the night and across the town and home to the robbers' house. And Aunt Sophia slept through it all.

Back at the robbers' house, the robbers carefully slung the hammock, complete with Sophia, between two hooks in the kitchen. Then they went into the adjoining room to go to bed.

"Good night," whispered Casper. "Good night," whispered Jesper. "It's going to be exciting when she wakes up," said Jonathan. He blew out the light. And soon they were fast asleep.

CHAPTER NINE—AUNT SOPHIA WAKES UP, BUT THINGS DON'T WORK OUT AS THE ROBBERS EXPECTED

Next morning, when the clock struck seven, Aunt Sophia awoke. She looked round in astonishment at the robbers' kitchen. "What a dreadful *mess!*" she exclaimed. She clambered out of the hammock and went into the adjoining room. Casper and Jesper and Jonathan were just getting up. They couldn't wait to see how things would go.

Miss Sophia fixed her eyes on the three robbers. "*Who* lives in this *rubbish* tip!" she demanded.

Casper plucked up courage and answered as boldly as he dared: "Dear—Miss—Sophia, *we* do."

"You do, do you? I might have guessed. Come here and introduce yourselves properly!"

Casper looked at the others: "We—we'd better do it," he said.
He took two steps forward and spoke up gruffly, like a man:
"Casper's the name!"

"Speak politely," said Sophia.

"I'll speak exactly as I like!" fumed Casper.

"You are never to answer a lady back in that fashion," frowned
Aunt Sophia sternly.

That made Casper angry: "I'll answer back exactly as I . . .
h'm."

"Next!" said Aunt Sophia. And Jesper stepped forward and
bowed politely.

"My name is Jesper," he said.

"Now, that's better," said Sophia.

"And I—I'm called Jonathan," said Jonathan stepping forward, with a dignified bow.

"So, you're the one they call Jonathan, are you? Come a bit closer. Let me see your ears."

"They're my own ears!" cried Jonathan in alarm.

"I can see that," said Sophia, "phoo, they're as black as soot. It's several years since you've washed *them!*"

Casper thought that was going too far: "Jonathan washes his ears when he decides!" he stormed.

"One glance is enough to tell me that," replied Miss Sophia.

She fixed her eyes for a moment on the three of them. Then she asked: "And *how* and *why* do I come to be here in this house?"

"Well, Miss Sophia—you see—" said Casper, "—you see, we—we've *stolen* you."

"Is that so? And do you think that's a fine thing to do?"

"Fine—or not, as the case may be," answered Casper. "The fact is, we need someone to keep house for us."

"And who can clean and tidy up," said Jesper.

"And who's good at preparing the kind of food we like," said Jonathan.

"And what were you thinking of doing?" asked Sophia.

"Ah," smiled Casper with a superior voice: "We plan to do exactly as we please."

"I see. You do, do you?"

"Yes, we do," answered the robbers in chorus.

Miss Sophia went round the house inspecting the mess that lay strewn about all over the place. "The house looks like a pigsty," she said.

"No, the pigsty's up the other end of the house," said Jesper.

"And how many pigs do you have there?" she asked.

"We only keep *one* pig," answered Jonathan.

"*One* there—and *three* here—that makes four!" said Sophia.

"What does she mean?" asked Casper painfully, looking across at the other two.

"She means us," whispered Jesper.

"It's just as I said, isn't it," said Jonathan, "she's an ogre."

But Casper pulled himself together: "*We're the ones who decide here!*" he said, vehemently.

"Yes, we're the ones," echoed Jesper and Jonathan.

Aunt Sophia looked at them in astonishment. "You, the one called Jesper—come here," she said.

Jesper didn't quite know what to do. He didn't want to do as she said, but he did it all the same.

"Do you see the mess strewn about everywhere?" asked Sophia.

"I see what I *want* to see," answered Jesper.

"Very well," said Sophia. "And now you'll tidy up all those clothes and whatever else you find lying about. Then you'll place Casper's things there, and Jonathan's things over there—and your things here."

"I can't tidy," said Jesper.

"Then you'll learn," said Sophia.

"Why can't Jonathan tidy up just as well?" said Jesper.

"Because there's another task for him," she answered.

Jonathan got up quietly and tried to sneak out of the door into the garden. But Miss Sophia's eyes caught him.

"Jonathan—come here!" she said.

"I *have* to go for a walk, that's all," said Jonathan.

"*You'll stay exactly where you are!*" said Sophia. "Collect all the cups and plates and knives and spoons. Then you can do the washing up!"

"Why can't Casper do that just as well?" said Jonathan.

"Because Casper has another job to do," answered Sophia.

"I don't do anything I don't want to do," protested Casper,

who by now was furious. But he didn't frighten Miss Aunt Sophia.

"Yes, that's right," she said. "You'll chop the wood—and get the oven going—and you'll boil the water for Jonathan to do the washing up."

"*He doesn't need any hot water for that!*" yelled Casper.

"Oh yes, he does," said Sophia. "And afterwards you'll boil up *more* water, and we'll use that for something else."

Casper and Jesper and Jonathan held back as long as they could. But it was no good saying *no*—because Aunt Sophia said *yes*. And while they got on with their jobs, she went round inspecting all three rooms. She scolded and she issued orders:

O fiddlesticks—o fiddlesticks! There's nothing here but bunk
and filth and dirt and nonsense stuff and every kind of junk.
But Jesper with a brush and pan will clear up all he can.
And afterwards he'll go outside and work with Jonathan!
    JESPER: No!   SOPHIA: Yes!

And Casper he can chop the wood and make the fire hot—
for we shall need an awful lot of water in the pot.
And Jonathan does washing up, there's nothing more to say.
And afterwards they'll go outside to wash and not to play.
    ROBBERS: No!   SOPHIA: Yes!

And Jonathan has dirty ears and doesn't hear a thing,
and Jesper's neck needs lots of soap to rid it of its ring.
And if he doesn't wash himself I'll lead a merry dance!
With scrub and brush I'll scrub his neck, he won't get one more
    chance.
    JESPER: No!   SOPHIA: Yes!

The robber men will learn to tidy everything in sight.
And no one slips away until the clock says nine at night!
I won't put up with rudeness if they dare to answer back.
And if they do what I decide they won't be in the black!
    ROBBERS: No!   SOPHIA: Yes!

Casper was making a great to-do over by the stove and it
looked as if he might have scalded himself because suddenly he
dropped a pot on the floor. "I can't see why we need all this hot
water!" he shouted.

"You're going to wash yourself," said Aunt Sophia. "And here's
the washbowl."

I don't *want* to wash," said Casper.

"That's all right," said Sophia, "then you won't get anything to eat. You will *not* sit down to table looking like that."

And even though he didn't want to, Casper had to fill the washbowl with water. And even though he didn't want to, he began to wash himself, timidly.

"Luckily, I'm not dirty," said Jesper.

"So you say," said Sophia. "Let me see your hands.—Fiddlesticks! Let me see your neck! That's right. Just as I thought. Get along with you and wash!" And she gave Jesper a prod in the direction of the washbowl.

At the sound of all this commotion the lion woke up and leaped down from the bed. Jesper gestured to the lion to bare his teeth and scare the strange little lady. He encouraged it by snarling and nudging the lion towards Aunt Sophia. The lion knew what Jesper wanted and began to growl and paw at her legs, pretending to be ferocious and dangerous.

But Aunt Sophia simply gave the lion a slap on the back of the head: "*Out of the way, house cat!*" she said, without so much as a by-your-leave. The lion leaped back in fright and slunk shame-facedly onto the bed again, while the robbers shook their heads in despair.

Jonathan tried to sneak off again, but Aunt Sophia caught him. "Jonathan!" she said, "weren't you thinking of washing yourself?"

"We can't all wash at once," answered Jonathan. But he had to give in as well. And the three of them dipped their hands into the washbowl and rubbed and scrubbed and moaned and groaned:

WASHING SONG

To wash ourselves—that's the most unpleasant yet.
Brushes are too rough, and water is too wet.
No, scrub and brush, soap and waterpan
are nothing proper for a robber man.

70

When, eventually, the robbers had made some pretence of washing both hands and faces, Aunt Sophia came out of the kitchen. This time she was a little kinder. First she glanced at Casper and then at Jesper and then at Jonathan. "Now, that's better," she said. "Now we can see what you're made of!"

The three robbers didn't answer, but just dried off the wet water. And Aunt Sophia started back for the kitchen—but just as she was going through the door she turned and said: "Now you can take off your boots and socks—and then you can wash your feet while I'm preparing the food."

But that incensed Casper: "We don't need to wash our feet to sit at the table!" he shouted. But he didn't get an answer, because Sophia had already shut the door.

"She didn't *hear* you," said Jonathan.

"She didn't *want* to hear," said Casper.

They didn't dare disobey Miss Sophia for none of them wanted to miss a meal. They poured more water into the washbowl and the three of them sat in a row on the bench, pulling and tugging to get their boots off.

"That's the stupidest thing we've ever carried off!" said Jesper.

"It's just as I said," sniffed Jonathan, "I told you she was an ogre."

"It was Casper's idea to have a lady housekeeper around the place," complained Jesper.

"Yes, but Jonathan's the one who thought of *carrying* her off."

"It wasn't me who thought of Miss Aunt Sophia," said Jonathan, close to tears.

"No, that was Casper," said Jesper.

"Well, what if it was!" answered Casper, petulantly. He stamped a foot into the washbowl, splashing water everywhere. The others just sat there looking miserable.

"I wish we were on our own again," sighed Jonathan.

71

"Me too," said Jesper. "We had a much better time before she came."

Then Casper had a bright idea: "Look," he said, "perhaps we could ask her to be so kind as to go back home!"

"Yes, we could certainly try," said Jesper.

"Then one of you'd better do it, I can't face her," said Jonathan.

"*I'll* see to it," said Casper, pulling himself together, for he was the eldest, after all. He pulled on his socks and boots, went to the kitchen and carefully knocked on the door—and opened it.

Aunt Sophia was standing over the stove making the food. She turned towards Casper and asked: "Do you need some more water?"

"No, no, no," answered a startled Casper. "That's not *it*. It—it was—something—else."

"Oh yes?" asked Sophia, waiting expectantly to hear what *it* was.

And Casper spoke as politely as he knew how: "Dear Miss Aunt Sophia," he said, "would you please be so kind as to go home again?"

"No!" answered Sophia, "now that I *am* here, I shall stay here."

"I see," said Casper looking down at the floor. "You—you can't *mean* that?" he said.

"Yes—I mean it."

"For pity's sake," said Jesper and Jonathan from the bench. They'd heard Sophia's answer. Casper made his way forlornly back to his seat, while Sophia carried on with her work.

That day, late in the afternoon, Jonathan stood gazing out of the window. Suddenly he gave a start. "Jumping jacks," he cried, "there's someone out there on the plain. There's three of them—with sticks and staffs!"

Casper rushed over and peered out. "It's the Police Inspector and another two," he said.

"So much the worse for us," said Jesper, dejectedly. But Jonathan was a bit more optimistic: "Perhaps—perhaps they've just come to fetch Miss Sophia."

"They're bound to arrest us at the same time," thought Casper. "Quick, lads—we'll hide as best as we can."

And Casper and Jesper and Jonathan hid behind the beds and the dressers. Meanwhile, the three who were approaching arrived at the robbers' house and marched up the steps leading to the door.

"Open up in the name of the law!" shouted Police Inspector Bastian, and rapped on the door with his truncheon. Rap, rap!

"Now, what's all the excitement?" asked Miss Sophia, making her way to the door and opening it, to find Inspector Bastian and

the pork butcher and the baker standing outside, holding long staffs.

"Thank goodness, we've found you, Miss Sophia," said Police Inspector Bastian, with relief.

"Oh?" said Sophia.

"We've come to rescue you from the robbers," said the pork butcher.

"Whatever for?" asked Sophia.

"Because you've been carried off by the robbers," said Bastian kindly. "But now you can return home with us, in safety."

"No, thank you," answered Sophia. "I'd prefer to stay here for the time being. I'm quite comfortable here. I like having someone to order about and knock some sense into."

The others looked at one another in astonishment.

"Do you *mean* that?" asked Bastian, in bewilderment.

"*That's* what I mean," answered Sophia.

"But what about the ferocious lion, Miss Sophia?" asked the baker.

"It isn't ferocious," answered Sophia.

"That's—remarkable," said the pork butcher.

"But—but in any event we have to arrest the robbers and take them to the police station with us," said Bastian.

"There's no need for that," said Aunt Sophia. "*I'll* take care of the robbers myself, Police Inspector. Just wait! I'll have them hard at work digging in the garden. They're going to grow vegetables and Cardamom pods and settle down like respectable folk."

"Well, well, well," said Police Inspector Bastian, who was only too pleased not to have to arrest anyone. "But—but then there's nothing more for us to do here," he said turning to the others.

"No, there isn't, after all," said the pork butcher.

"Well, well," said Bastian, "then we'll be off. Good day, good day!"

And so the baker and the pork butcher and Police Inspector Bastian set off home to Cardamom Town.

Inside their robbers' den the three robbers had been listening. They'd heard every word, and they were alarmed, to say the least.

"She didn't *want* to go home," said Casper.

"What a calamity," said Jesper.

"Did you hear what she said," said Jonathan. "*I'll have them hard at work digging*—did you hear that?"

"And growing vegetables and Cardamom pods," said Casper. "She really thinks she, she can . . ."

"But she saved us from being arrested," said Jesper.

"I'd rather be arrested than stay here in the house with her," said Jonathan.

"Something has to be done," said Casper.

Then the three of them sat on the bench for what seemed hours and thought about what could be done. And finally it dawned on one of them, and that was Jonathan: "Lads," he said, "*I think I have a plan!*"

"What's the plan?" asked Casper eagerly.

"Listen carefully," whispered Jonathan, looking round to make sure Miss Sophia was out of earshot: "*Tonight—when Miss Sophia's sleeping we'll carry her back to where we carried her off from!*"

"That's a wonderful plan!" said Casper.

"You're a smart one," said Jesper.

"I guess so," said Jonathan.

Then the three of them danced a happy robbers' dance and Aunt Sophia opened the door to see what the three of them were up to.

That night, when the house was quiet and Miss Sophia was sound asleep in the hammock, Casper and Jesper and Jonathan entered the room, carefully lifted the hammock off its hooks, and carried Miss Aunt Sophia out of the robbers' house, all the way across the plain, into town, and home to the house from where they'd carried her off. And Aunt Sophia slept through it all.

Jonathan opened the door cautiously and Casper and Jesper crept into the kitchen and hung the hammock back in its place, while Jonathan stood watch outside. Before long, Casper and Jesper came out again. "Did it go according to plan?" asked Jonathan.

"All according to plan," said Casper. "Miss Aunt Sophia's back where she belongs—without being woken," said Jesper.

"We're a smart bunch," said Jonathan.

"Yes, we're pretty smart," said Casper. "Hurrah!"

And then they made their way home again to the robbers'
house, singing their happy song:

THE HAPPY ROBBERS

Now we will head for home again
and live a life that's freer.
Now we will have a lovely time,
for we have ditched Sophia.
And never wash and be uncouth,
and never brush a single tooth.
No, now we will clean just as little we can—
both Casper and Jesper and Jonathan.
   "Yes, that'll be a new life, that!"

And we won't wash the dishes up,
for that's not necessary.
The water in our wishing well
we do not wish to carry.
No, scrub and soap and waterpan
are nothing for a robber man.
No, now we will wash just as little we can—
both Casper and Jesper and Jonathan.
   "And that'll be little, that!"

And we will never chop the wood,
and never light the fire.
And never have a lady maid
whatever we require.
And we will mess up all we can
and never use a brush and pan.
For now we will do just as little we can—
both Casper and Jesper and Jonathan.
   "Yes, that's what we'll do."

CHAPTER TEN—THE SECRET ABOUT OLD TOBIAS IN THE TOWER

The day after the expedition to the robbers' house to rescue Aunt Sophia, Police Inspector Bastian was out on his usual morning stroll through the town, when he met little Remo.

"Police Inspector," said Remo, "shall I tell you a secret?"

"What sort of a secret is that, then?" asked Bastian.

"Tobias is seventy-five years old today!"

"No, that can't be possible," said Bastian, "Old Tobias all of seventy-five?"

"Yes, it is possible. He told me so himself when I visited him yesterday. Tomorrow I'll be an old man, because then I'll be seventy-five, that's what he said. And tomorrow yesterday must be today today, mustn't it?"

79

Bastian thought for a moment. "Yes—yes it most assuredly is. But then we have to do something extra special!"

"We ought to give him something," said Remo.

"We certainly should," said Bastian. "And we ought to make a speech."

"And the Town Orchestra could play a celebration march," said barber Patterson who'd overheard the secret as he stood on his step.

"We really ought to compose a song, too," thought Bastian, "we ought to . . ."

Just then Aunt Sophia passed by. Police Inspector Bastian gazed at her in amazement. He didn't know Sophia had been carried off back during the night. "But—Miss Aunt Sophia," he said, "are you here? I thought . . ."

"I *am* where I *am!*" said Aunt Sophia.

"Yes, *that* you are," said Bastian. "By the way, did you know Tobias is seventy-five years old today?"

"Oh, yes, is that all he is?" said Sophia.

"Old Tobias—" said Bastian, "is a very likeable man."

"More likeable than most," said Sophia, whatever she meant by that. "Anyway, we must give him something," she said.

"That's just what we were talking about," said Bastian. "The question is: *what* shall we give him?"

"He could do with an alarm clock, then he might forecast the weather for us a little earlier in the day," said Aunt Sophia.

"He really ought to have a special present, something that'll give him great joy and boundless pleasure," thought barber Patterson.

"Perhaps he'd like a pet," suggested Remo, "one he could talk to, so it wouldn't be so sad and lonely for him up there."

"That's not a bad idea," agreed Bastian. "If the pet shop's open we can go along straight away and see what the pet dealer has in stock."

"Yes, you do that," said barber Patterson. "Meanwhile, I'll go over to tram driver Puddleson's and ask him to compose a suitable hurrah song."

"Splendid," said Bastian. "And let's hope we can buy a cuddly pet."

"Everyone has to contribute," said Aunt Sophia.

"Yes, everyone," said Bastian.

The pet dealer was in the square outside his shop when Police Inspector Bastian and Remo and Aunt Sophia arrived. He was in the middle of teaching his horse how to dance. It was a pretty little horse, which answered to the name Hippocrates. The pet dealer was dancing in front of the horse, demonstrating some steps.

Trip the light fantastic with four legs down and tail high—
hey ho hop Hippocrates.
Chest pushed out and belly taut and supple limbs will fly—
hey ho hop Hippocrates.
Bare your lovely teeth—and turn your head a bit askew.
Watch the steps I take and try to follow what I do.
Afterwards there's sugar lumps and timothy grass to chew—
hey ho hop Hippocrates.

"What's this?" asked Bastian enthusiastically.

"It's Hippocrates—my newest horse," replied the pet dealer.

"Why is he hopping about?" asked Aunt Sophia.

"He's not hopping—he's dancing," said the pet dealer proudly. "He's practising for next year's Cardamom fête."

Bastian nodded enthusiastically: "A very good number!"

"Never mind that," said Aunt Sophia. "We've come to look for a pet."

"You see, old Tobias is seventy-five today," explained Bastian, "so we thought of making a collection for a present, and we thought we might give him an animal!"

"Because Tobias is very fond of animals!" said Remo.

"A jolly good idea," said the pet dealer. "A pet is just the thing to give old Tobias. A little acrobatic animal, a little songbird—they're all here. Large animals and little animals, birds and fish!"

"We could buy a parrot," suggested Remo, "because he could talk to and be talked back to by a parrot."

"That's not such a bad idea," said Police Inspector Bastian.

The pet dealer was keen too: "It so happens I've got just the parrot Tobias would like. Over there. Quite a rare specimen. Talks—sings—exceptionally clever."

"Let's hear what it can do, then," said Aunt Sophia.

"With the greatest of pleasure!" And the pet dealer fetched the parrot. "Polly," he said, "would you tell these kind folk who you *are*—and where you come from."

And the parrot nodded its head and sang:

THE PRETTY POLLY FROM AMERICA

I am a pretty polly from America.
The far off country of my patronymic.
At first I couldn't talk but said my pretty polly ma:
His ABC he'll quickly come to mimic.
And so I can—o falderee o faldera,
if someone asks me if I come from far,
I answer falderee o faldera—
I am a pretty polly from America.

The forest was my home till I was eight years old.
But then the pretty polly catcher caught me.
I learnt to talk and understand from everything he told,
and many catchy melodies he taught me.

84

And so I can—o falderee o faldera.
If someone asks who taught me my sol-fa,
I answer falderee o faldera—
the pretty polly catcher in America.

One day there came a captain and he purchased me,
my cabin was the captain's biggest pocket.
We sailed the sea, but I jumped ship in order to be free,
in Cardamom I'm more than just a house pet.
And here I am—o falderee o faldera,
and here in town I'm something of a star.
And they all know—o falderee o faldera—
that I am pretty polly from America.

"What a magnificent parrot!" said Police Inspector Bastian.
"Just the thing for Tobias," said Remo.
"How much does it cost?" asked Aunt Sophia.
"It's priced at eighty pounds," replied the pet dealer.
"That's expensive!" said Sophia.
"Yes, but I'll contribute to the collection myself," said the pet dealer.
"Yes, everyone will," said Aunt Sophia.
Just then barber Patterson returned. "Everything's arranged!" he said. "I've spoken to tram driver Puddleson. He's writing a splendid little hurrah song. And swimming and music instructor Anderson is composing a brand new hurrah melody."
"That's terrific news," said Police Inspector Bastian. "And here's the pet."
"I must say that's a fine specimen," said Patterson.
"Talks—sings—exceptionally clever," said the pet dealer.
"We'll buy it," said Aunt Sophia. So *that* was decided.

CHAPTER ELEVEN—IN WHICH OLD TOBIAS'S BIRTHDAY IS CELEBRATED WITH SPEECHES AND PRESENTS AND HURRAH SONGS

When, a little later that day, old Tobias looked out from his tower and saw so many flags in the distance and heard music, he wondered what kind of a day it could be today. It wasn't Easter and it wasn't Whitsun, and Cardamom Day had just gone. Then he gave a knowing smile and winked an eye: "It can't be because it's my birthday today?"

But *that's* just what it was! While Tobias was up in his tower, looking out over the town, all his friends were walking down the street with flags and flowers, in high spirits, led by the Cardamom Town Orchestra, wearing white caps, with flowers in their buttonholes. Grown ups and little ones were waving and shouting hurrah. That's when Tobias realized the music and the flags and everything else were meant for him. And he felt very pleased indeed.

When everyone was assembled in front of the tower house, Police Inspector Bastian took the stand and made a fine birthday speech in honour of their good friend:

"Dear Tobias," he said. "You are the best and kindest and wisest inhabitant of Cardamom Town. Which is why we've bought you a special present. It's from all of us, and it's a parrot! We know you'll be pleased with it. It can talk and sing. And if you listen carefully up in your tower you'll hear it sing a song—about itself—for you. Polly, if you please!"

And the pretty polly from America sang about the life of a polly, and everyone applauded both the parrot and Bastian's splendid speech. Bastian gave the parrot cage to Tommy, and Tommy ran upstairs to the top of the tower and presented the cage and the parrot to Tobias.

But there were several presents. Little Remo had brought along a basket with something inside. And Remo made a fine speech, too:

"Dear Tobias! I want to give you a present, too. It's Bobby's prettiest puppy. It's yours because you're always so kind. It's here in the basket, and I'm coming up with it now!"

Old Tobias was so happy standing in his tower house with the parrot cage in one hand—and the basket holding the puppy in the other.

"My dear friends," he said. "I'm so filled with joy and happiness I could almost cry. I've always wanted two things. A little puppy, and a delightful parrot to talk to. And now both wishes have come true on the very same day. A thousand thanks!"

Everyone applauded and shouted hurrah. And tram driver Puddleson stepped forward with a large billboard, and on the billboard were the words of the birthday song.

"And now," said Police Inspector Bastian, "we'll all sing our new hurrah song, written in honour of you, Tobias, on this momentous day. One—two—three!"

HURRAH SONG FOR TOBIAS

We will sing our hurrah song and play—hurrah hurrah!
for a man with a birthday today—hurrah hurrah!
For Tobias who lives in our town—in our town,
with a tower house from where he looks down—
   he looks down.
He makes only happy friendships,
it is his hat he always tips
when he greets everyone in our town—hurrah hurrah!

He is bearded and ancient and wise—hurrah hurrah!
And to questions he always replies—hurrah hurrah!
He's the wisest of all in our town—in our town,
and his forecasts will not let us down—let us down.
For Tobias on the balcony
and the seventy-five he'll be
we will shout out a hearty hurrah—hurrah hurrah!

CHAPTER TWELVE—IN WHICH TOMMY LIVES THROUGH AN EXCITING EXPERIENCE

The day after Tobias's seventy-fifth birthday, Tommy went out for a ride on his donkey. He rode out through the town gate and across the plain. The weather was fine and Pontius trotted along peacefully while Tommy sat on the donkey's back, whistling contentedly and thinking about nothing in particular.

Then suddenly—far away from the town—Tommy caught sight of a peculiar old house, out on the plain. This was new territory for Tommy, and he'd never set eyes on the house before. He wondered who lived there—and *if* anyone lived there.

He tethered Pontius to a tree, crept up to the house and peered through a grimy window. Inside, he saw an enormous lion lying asleep in an old bed. "How peculiar," said Tommy to himself. He crept on a bit and peered through another window. Inside, he saw three unshaven characters moving about and bickering with

one another, surrounded by a pile of rubbish. They were searching through drawers and cupboards.

Tommy realized the three characters were the robbers Casper
and Jesper and Jonathan.

"I can't find any bread," said the one known as Casper.

"There isn't any bread to find," said Jonathan.

"D'you mean there's not a loaf in the house?" asked Casper,
who seemed to hanker after bread.

"Not so much as a crispbread," said Jesper.

"Not so much as a gingerbread," said Jonathan.

"Well, well," said Casper. "We'll just have to go out robbing
tonight!"

"That makes sense on several counts," said Jonathan. "We
need a little of everything—as a matter of fact."

Then they discussed *when* they would start out—and what
they needed most—and where they would start out for first.

All this and more Tommy heard as he stood outside the window. But he didn't dare stay any longer for fear the robbers
would discover him. So he crept away from the robbers' house,
mounted his donkey and rode back to town as fast as he could.

When Tommy arrived home, he told his father, grocer Hill,
what he'd discovered. His father was most alarmed because the
robbers had broken into his shop on many occasions and stolen
things like sugar and coffee and split peas and groats. Grocer Hill
fetched the baker and the pork butcher, and Tommy had to
recount everything he'd seen and heard.

"I was riding Pontius across the plain," Tommy began. "Then
I saw a peculiar old tall house. I wonder who lives there, I
thought. So I left Pontius tethered, crept up to the house and
peered in through a grimy window, where I saw a lion lying
asleep in a bed."

"That was the robbers' house," said the pork butcher.

"I peered in through another window," said Tommy, "and saw

the three robbers. The one called Casper, the other called Jesper, and the little tubby one called Jonathan."

"What were the robbers doing?" asked grocer Hill.

"They seemed to be going round searching high and low for something, because the place was in an awful mess. And then the one called Casper said: I can't find any bread. There isn't any bread to find, said the one called Jonathan."

"What did Casper say then?" asked the baker.

"We'll have to go out robbing tonight. And then Jonathan said: That makes sense on several counts because we need a little of everything, as a matter of fact."

"And then?" asked grocer Hill.

"Well, then Casper said: First we'll pay a visit to the baker. And then we'll pay a visit to the pork butcher."

"What did the others say then?" asked the pork butcher.

"Hurrah for the pork butcher, they said."

"They said that, did they?"

The baker became particularly alarmed, but the pork butcher gestured excitedly: "Now we can capture the robbers, at last," he said. "All we have to do is to hide in the bakery, and then we'll catch the three of them. And when we've caught them we'll hand them over to the Police Inspector."

"Wouldn't it be better to catch them in the pork butcher's shop?" asked the baker.

"We'll catch them in the bakery because that's where they're going first," said the pork butcher.

But the baker was shaking a bit at the knees. He wasn't feeling that courageous. "Wouldn't it be best to have Police Inspector Bastian along?" he asked.

"That's not necessary," said the pork butcher. "We're three men, and they're three robbers. That's exactly one robber for each one of us. And you, grocer Hill, you capture the biggest, I'll capture the middlemost—and you baker, you capture the smallest."

"Right," said grocer Hill. "Er—right," said the baker.

"If everything's clear, let's go and hide in the bakery. And you, Tommy, you must go home."

"Yes, but it was me who explained everything," said Tommy.

"Never mind that, Tommy," said grocer Hill, "you go home to bed, because this could be dangerous!"

"That's not fair at all!" said Tommy.

Reluctantly, he mounted Pontius and rode home in a huff, while the others hid themselves inside and outside the bakery and waited for the robbers to show themselves.

CHAPTER THIRTEEN—IN WHICH CASPER AND JESPER AND JONATHAN GO TO TOWN ON A ROBBING SPREE

The three robbers knew nothing of the plans laid by the pork butcher and the baker and grocer Hill. They sat at home in their robbers' house, hankering after bread and waiting for nightfall.

"I'd better give the lion a bite to eat before we set out," said Jesper.

"You can give him that leftover meatloaf," said Casper.

Jesper fetched the meat and went into the adjoining room where the lion lay resting in the bed. It snarled a bit, as lions do when they're hungry.

"Here's some meatloaf," said Jesper. The lion ate the meat with gusto, and washed it down with a bucket of water. Well and truly satisfied, the lion padded over and buried his head in

Jesper's lap. Jesper scratched the lion behind the ear, because the lion particularly liked that.

"What a lovely lion, you are," said Jesper. "Mm," said the lion.

"You'll make sure no one ever comes and takes away your old friend Jesper, won't you?" "M-m," said the lion.

"That's good," said Jesper, and gave the beast a long, slow scratch. And then the lion gave a sort of yawn, and then Jesper gave a sort of yawn—and they both fell asleep.

Meanwhile night fell. It grew dark, and the other two wondered what had become of Jesper.

"I haven't seen him for ages," said Casper.

"He went in to feed the lion with the meatloaf," said Jonathan. "What if the lion thought it wasn't enough . . . ?"

"You mean the lion might . . . ?"

"Yes, exactly," said Jonathan. "You can never be sure with lions."

"We'd better take a look," said Casper.

They went into the room next door. There lay the lion and Jesper—both of them—asleep in the bed.

"Oh, look how sweet they are," said Jonathan.

But Casper shook Jesper. "Up you get," he said. "It's time to go robbing."

And Jesper sat up like a shot. "What time is it?" he asked.

"It's time enough," said Casper.

"Are we taking the lion along?" asked Jesper.

"No—no lion," said Casper. "It'll only make a noise."

"It might be best if we had him with us, in case anyone tries to capture us," said Jonathan.

"There can't be anyone expecting us to come just this evening," said Casper.

So they locked the door of the robbers' house and set off, happily and cheerfully, because soon they'd have all the bread they wanted.

ROBBERS' SONG

We sneak on tiptoe as we go
so stealthily to steal-o.
We take just what we need and know
where we can find a meal-o.
Now darkness lies upon the town,
asleep beneath its eiderdown.
We're off with our bag and our bucket and pan,
both Casper and Jesper and Jonathan.

The butcher smokes a hock of ham
and cervelat and bacon;
loin of pork and rack of lamb,
to feed the lion, we've taken.
A rib of beef for roasting rare,
and sausages are spicy fare.
But then we make do just as best as we can,
both Casper and Jesper and Jonathan.

The baker shop is where we stop,
we shan't pinch much from there though,
just bread and cake and soda pop,
enough for us to share-o.
It's true that sometimes Jonathan
will grab himself a gingerman.
But then we make do just as best as we can,
both Casper and Jesper and Jonathan.
        (Yes, that's what we do.)

The town was silent and in darkness as Casper and Jesper and
Jonathan stole through the town gate, along the street, making
straight for the bakery.

"We must take care not to wake the baker," said Casper. "We

THE BAKERY

mustn't make any noise," said Jonathan. And Jesper brought out his bunch of keys to find the one that fitted. But when he took hold of the door handle, the door opened of its own accord.

"How about that!" said Jesper, "the baker forgot to lock the door." "Lucky for us," said Casper. "Then we can just walk straight in," said Jonathan.

It was dark inside the bakery, but the robbers knew where the bread and the cakes were kept. Casper opened his sack and placed in it seven, no, eight brown loaves and yeast cakes and farmhouse whites and a little of everything. Jesper grabbed a large bar of dairy milk chocolate. While Jonathan found a whole crate of biscuits. "Gingersnaps!" he exclaimed with barely concealed glee. "Sh!" said Casper.

And suddenly the door slammed behind them, the light went on, and they heard a furious and fearsome voice: "Caught in the act—the lot of you!"

There stood the pork butcher, the baker and grocer Hill. Casper, rooted to the spot, stared at the three robber catchers.

96

"This is too bad!" he said.

"It's just as I thought," said Jesper, "we should have brought the lion with us."

"This is calamitous," said Jonathan, "just as everything was turning out so well."

"Are you going to give yourselves up freely?" asked the pork butcher.

Casper turned to the others: "What d'you think, lads?"

"It looks as if we'll have to," said Jesper. And Jonathan said: "If I can take along a bag of gingersnaps, I'll give myself up."

"Yes, take the bag then," said the baker.

"Thank you very much," said Jonathan.

"Baker, do you have a stout rope?" asked the pork butcher. "A long one, preferably!"

"How stupid of us to come here just today," said Jesper.

"Yes," said Jonathan, "and it was Casper who . . ."

"It was *you* who ate up all the bread and stuff," fumed Casper.

The baker returned with a long rope, and they tied the robbers together one behind the other.

"I can't imagine what's the point of that," said Casper, irritated.

"It's to make sure you don't run off once we're outside," said the pork butcher.

"But suppose they run off with the rope and all?" said grocer Hill.

"That wouldn't be so amusing," said the pork butcher.

"I know what we can do," said the baker. "I can tie you both to the rope, together with the robbers—one in front and one behind, then the robbers won't be able to run off."

"That's clever, baker," said the pork butcher.

And so they were tied too—the pork butcher to the front of the rope and grocer Hill to the end of the rope. And that's how they marched, crocodile fashion, through the town and straight to the police station.

When they arrived at the police station the baker went up to the door and knocked. Knock, knock, knock! It took a little time for Police Inspector Bastian to wake up, but after a while they heard his voice inside: "Who is it?" he demanded.

"It's the three robbers," said the baker.

"What on earth—*what do you want here?*"

"It's the baker knocking, Police Inspector. We've captured the robbers."

"That's impossible!"

"No, it's quite possible," said the baker. "Open up and you'll see."

And Bastian opened the door and came out onto the step, holding a lamp.

"Here are the robbers," said the baker, proudly.

"Yes, but—yes, but, there seem to be five of them," said Bastian in astonishment.

"There's only three, Mr Bastian. The other two are the pork butcher and grocer Hill."

"Yes, of course, now I can see. Good morning, pork butcher, my man—good morning, grocer Hill—or good *night*, I should say, because that's *what* it is, isn't it?" Then they all laughed.

"And welcome to you," said Bastian turning to the robbers. "Be so good as to take off your—the rope, I mean, while I fetch the case report ledger."

Police Inspector Bastian fetched his spectacles and the large book he called the case report ledger, and sat down at the table.

"You're the three robbers, then," he said.

"Yes," said the robbers.

"I have to write that down," said Bastian, writing in his book.

"And what are your names?" he asked.

"Casper," said Casper. "Jesper," said Jesper. "And my name's Jonathan," said Jonathan. And Bastian wrote that down in his book too.

"And what wrongdoing have you done?" he asked.

The three robbers looked at one another. "You tell," said Jonathan to Casper. And Casper began: "We—we were just out for an evening stroll—and then it grew so cold—and then our fingers were so frozen—and so—so we thought the baker had just baked some bread—and then the bakery's such a warm and cosy place, we thought—and so we just wanted to go in and warm ourselves up a bit."

"H'm," said Bastian, "that doesn't sound so preposterous."

"Yes, but what he's saying isn't true," said the baker. "The three robbers went into the bakery to steal bakery goods, and that

big one already had eight brown loaves, two yeast cakes and three farmhouse whites stuffed in his sack."

"That's not so good," said Bastian. "What have you to say to that?"

"Well," said Casper, "that was just a little mishap. When we went into the bakery it was so dark inside—and I had my sack in my hand—and the sack was open. And then I bumped slap bang into a shelf, and the shelf was stacked with brown loaves and white bread and yeast cakes, and they fell down off the shelf— slap bang into my sack."

Bastian looked up at the others: "That doesn't sound so completely preposterous either?"

"But it's not true!" said the baker, "because the browns and the whites aren't stored on the same shelf."

"Aren't they, indeed! This looks bad." Bastian eyed Casper

101

sadly: "So, is it true that you *did*, in fact, set out to rob the baker of his bread?"

"*Yes, well, that's what we did, then,*" said Casper.

"Wait a moment," said Bastian, "I have to write that down. Can you say that *once* more."

"Yes—well—that's—what—we—did, then," said Casper. And Bastian wrote it down: "what—we—did—then."

"The podgy one there had his mouth full of gingersnaps when we caught him!" said the pork butcher, pointing at Jonathan.

"Is that true?" asked Bastian.

"Yes," answered Jonathan.

"That's because he's very fond of gingersnaps," said Casper.

And Bastian wrote: "fond—of—gingersnaps. Right, then. Did you take anything else?"

"No," answered Casper.

"It could be there's something in their pockets," said grocer Hill.

"No, that couldn't be," said Casper.

"Well, well, perhaps you'd make a search, grocer Hill." And Hill felt the robbers' pockets, first Casper's, then Jonathan's and then Jesper's.

"I haven't got anything," said Casper.

"I've only got a bag of gingernuts, and I was given them," said Jonathan.

"That's correct," said the baker.

"But, but, but—look at this, Police Inspector! A large bar of milk chocolate." Grocer Hill held up the chocolate so Police Inspector Bastian could see it.

"So, now. Milk chocolate?" questioned Bastian.

"Yes, but it's not for me," said Jesper.

"Who's it *for* then?"

"It's for the lion."

"What's that! Milk chocolate for a lion?"

"Yes," said Jesper, "dairy milk chocolate is its favourite."

"Yes, yes," said Bastian, "it's good of you to be so considerate to animals, even a lion. *But it's not good to steal!*"

"I know it's not," said Jesper, "and I meant to pay when the baker came, but I didn't have time to, because he came in so quickly."

"Yes, yes," said Bastian, "that was this time. But you've been to town many times *before* on your robbing sprees—and that's why I'm arresting you *in the name of the law.*—You'll spend forty-eight days in jail."

"That's a long time!" said Casper.

"Yes, but you'll get a comfortable room."

"Is it warm in there?" asked Jesper.

"Cosy and warm," said Bastian.

"Do we get food as well?" asked Jonathan.

"You'll get that. Three times a day."

"Then it's not so bad," said Jonathan.

And the case was closed.

"Ah, yes, that's that," said the pork butcher. "And now we can go home again, can't we?"

"Yes, you can," said Bastian. "And many thanks for the robbers!"

"Oh—the pleasure's all ours," said the baker.

The three robber catchers said goodnight to the robbers and to Police Inspector Bastian, and went home to lie down and get some sleep, safe and sound in their beds. And Police Inspector Bastian opened the cell door.

"Well then, robbers! It's in *here* you have to go," he said. "You'll be staying right here. It's a little untidy just at the moment, but you'll have to take it as it is. Nobody's lived in it for quite some while."

And so the three robbers were locked up in the jail—which was situated in the same building as the police station.

CHAPTER FIFTEEN—CASPER AND JESPER AND JONATHAN IN JAIL

The jail had only one cell, a big room, but it was light and airy and cosy—with beds and table and chairs. Early the next morning, Mrs Bastian brought them breakfast and coffee. It tasted marvellous to the robbers after the night's exertions. A little later, Police Inspector Bastian came in as well, refreshed and cheerful.

"Now, robbers," he said, "have you slept well?"

"We've slept very well," said Casper and Jesper and Jonathan.

"The beds are comfortable," said Casper.

"The chairs are comfortable too," said Jesper.

"And now we've had a delicious breakfast," said Jonathan.

"That's good to hear," said Bastian. "And now I'm off to grocer Hill to buy you a washbowl and a scrubbing brush and some soap."

"Dear Police Inspector, there's absolutely no need for that,"

said Casper and Jesper and Jonathan. "We're quite all right as we are."

"Yes, yes," said Bastian, "but a little soap and water won't hurt. I'll be back shortly."

Just then Mrs Bastian came in, carrying flowers in a vase. "Now, look at that!" said Police Inspector Bastian, "there's even flowers for you!"

"It's only a few marguerites and some wild sprigs," said Mrs Bastian. "We must try to make it bit cosier in here. Was the food to your liking?"

The three of them got up from the table and bowed. "It was very much to our liking," they answered. "Thank you very much for the food, Mrs Bastian!"

"You're welcome. And now perhaps you'll help me a little and make the beds, while I clear the table."

"We'll do that with the greatest of pleasure," said Casper and Jesper and Jonathan. Immediately, they began straightening sheets and quilts and pillows. "Just let us know, Mrs Bastian, if there's anything we can do to help," said Casper. "We'd be glad to," said Jonathan.

And while the robbers made their beds, Mrs Bastian cleared the table, and set the flowers in the centre, all the while singing a little song:

MRS BASTIAN'S SONG

I tidy and I straighten—and keep things spick and span.
And Superintendent Bastian—he is the sweetest man.
My husband really is a peach, he is so kind and fair,
and when I do the washing up, the drying is his share.

He keeps the peace and order—in Cardamom our town.
But Casper and Jesper and Jonathan have only let him down.
He's taken them in custody—that's how it has to be.
Before we had no prisoners here—but now we have these three.

But all of them are courteous—and no one picks a fight.
They say they're enjoying a good time here—that prison is all
  right.
They find it much more comfortable—than in their bachelors'
  pad.
And I can hardly think that they—are really quite so bad.

A bit unkempt and scruffy—but we have had a chat.
A brush and a comb and a mild shampoo—will surely see to that.
And when they've washed their matted hair—and look the best
  they can,
such handsome men will reappear—especially Jonathan.

107

Meanwhile, Police Inspector Bastian had paid a visit to grocer Hill, and now he was back with the washing things. "Look, here's the washbowl," he said, "and there's a pitcher of water, and here's the scrubbing brush and the hair brush and some soap!"

Casper tried to protest once more: "That's completely unnecessary," he urged.

But Mrs Bastian smiled and said: "We'll put the wash things over here in the corner, then you can wash yourselves when you feel like it."

"And if you need some more water," said Bastian, "just give a shout." And then Mr and Mrs Bastian left, leaving the robbers to themselves again.

"We're having a pretty comfortable time here, really," said Jesper.

"Yes, we are," said Casper. "It's almost as if we were respectable folk."

"It almost makes me feel like having a bit of a wash and brush up," said Jonathan.

"That's how I feel, too," said Jesper.

"Washing's kids' stuff," said Casper—"but seeing as Mrs Bastian's so kind, then . . ."

"Then, all the same, perhaps we ought to try it a bit," said Jonathan—"just a tiny little bit—wash a bit, I mean."

Then they poured some water into the washbowl, and soon the three of them were washing.

THE ROBBERS' WASHING SONG

To wash ourselves that's the most unpleasant yet,
brushes are too rough, and water is too wet.
No, scrub and brush, soap and waterpan
are nothing proper for a robber man.

But—Mr and Mrs Bastian are quite a special pair,
which is why we'd like to wash and brush our hair.
We want to be just as clean as we can
here in the house of Mr Bastian.

They washed themselves thoroughly. Jesper dipped the whole
of his head into the bowl, splashing soapy water everywhere. And
Casper even washed his ears.

"I'm beginning to think it feels great to be clean, after all," said
Jesper.

"Yes," said Casper, "and I seem to be able to hear better afterwards."

"My, don't we look handsome," said Jonathan, admiring himself in the mirror.

Yes, they'd turned out so handsome they were hardly recognizable. Even Police Inspector Bastian had some difficulty when he came in a little later to see how they were getting on.

"But—but, he can't be one of you, surely?" he mused.

"Yes," said Casper, "that's one of us, because that's Jesper."

"He's only washed himself," said Jonathan. And then the four of them burst out laughing.

"Yes, we're enjoying ourselves here, Police Inspector," said Casper.

"I'm glad to hear it," said Bastian.

"And then it's a great thing to be able to talk to other people," said Jesper. "Up to now, we've only really spoken to one another, never to anyone else."

"That's true," said Casper.

"And what a luxury it is to have meals prepared by a lady," said Jonathan.

"Yes, Mrs Bastian is very kind," said Casper. And Police Inspector Bastian certainly agreed with him on that score.

"There's just *one* thing I'm feeling sad about," said Jesper, "and I can't stop thinking about it. While we're here enjoying ourselves the poor lion's lying at home in our house hungry."

"That's not so good," said Bastian.

"Couldn't you be so kind as to arrest him as well?" asked Jesper.

At the thought of that, Police Inspector Bastian became quite alarmed.

"*That*, I'm afraid, is *completely* out of the question," he said. "A lion isn't the sort of animal one can arrest."

"He's quite a softy," said Jesper.

But Bastian was resolute. "A lion is a lion," he affirmed. "It will have to stay out at the robbers' house until you return home. But Jesper has permission to make a trip once a day with some food, that's the answer."

"I haven't any food for the lion," said Jesper.

But Bastian promised to rustle up some lion feed. "I'll talk with the baker and the pork butcher," he said, "and they're sure to let me have a few meat bones and some old crusts of bread."

Half an hour later he was back with a whole sackful of lion feed. There was meat from the pork butcher—and stale bread from the baker. "And look, here's a bar of dairy milk chocolate for the lion, and that's from me," said Bastian.

So Jesper was allowed out for a few hours and went off to the robbers' house with food for the lion. He came back that evening. "The lion ate it all up almost in one go," he reported. "And he was very pleased with the chocolate."

"That's splendid," said Police Inspector Bastian.

CHAPTER SIXTEEN—IN WHICH BARBER PATTERSON IS PLEASANTLY SURPRISED

After the robbers had washed themselves, and spruced themselves up a little, they looked quite handsome. But Bastian still thought they had a little too much hair and were too unshaven in appearance. And one day he sent a message to barber Patterson asking him to stop by and cut the robbers' hair and trim their whiskers.

"Police Inspector, Sir! There's no need for that," protested Casper. "We like having our hair as it is—and our stubble . . ."

But just as he was talking, who should step through the door but barber Patterson with scissors and comb and brush. And he had his clarinet with him, as well. Because barber Patterson was not only able to cut and shave, he was a member of the Cardamom Town Orchestra, and played and sang whenever there was a moment to spare.

"Yes, here are the dear robbers," said Bastian. "This is Casper—Jesper—and Jonathan. Perhaps you'd care to give them a neat trim, barber, while I go into town and fetch some lion feed."

Barber Patterson greeted the robbers cheerfully and gave their hair the once-over. "Ah, yes," he said—"Casper parted on the right side—Jesper parted on the left side—and Jonathan . . ."

"I don't *have* any parting, me," said Jonathan, "and I haven't had one for years."

"Well, well—then we'll do Jonathan first," said Patterson.

But Jonathan was apprehensive: "Couldn't we do Casper first, instead, because he's the biggest?" he asked.

"No, Jonathan first," said Casper. "That's best."

"That's always best, isn't it," said Jonathan. But he sat down on the chair, anyway, and barber Patterson tied a white sheet round him so that he wouldn't get hair all over his clothes.

Barber Patterson had quite a difficult job with the three robbers' hair, for it was very tousled and tangled and knotted. "Ow, ow!" said Jonathan. But when Patterson had cut and brushed and combed the three of them, the robbers were so pleased with themselves they couldn't stop gazing into the mirror.

"No one would believe that was Casper," said Casper.

"No one would believe that was Jesper, either," said Jesper.

"And no one would believe I'm Jonathan," said Jonathan.

Now the hard work was done, barber Patterson was free to take out his clarinet and play and sing his little song:

THE MASTER BARBER'S SONG

I wash and cut and shape the hair of townsfolk all day long.
But best of all I like to play a music singalong.
In Cardamom Town Orchestra I am the leading man,
and try to play my clarinet as often as I can.
    (Clarinet solo)

113

And when Tobias pays a visit to my barbershop,
I wash his long white whiskers from the bottom to the top.
And while his beard is left to dry I take my clarinet,
and sitting down beside him, play a tune he won't forget.
 (Clarinet solo)

To play my notes is all I want, I do it all day long,
and while I cut and clip I sing my master barber song.
I trim a beard and shave a chin and no one gets upset
because I sing my barber song, and play my clarinet.
 (Clarinet solo)

When the song and the music were over, the robbers clapped their hands. "You can certainly play, I must say," said Casper.

"Is there anyone here who's good at playing?" asked barber Patterson.

"Yes, *we* are," said Casper.

The barber was surprised. "Can you really play?" he asked.

"Oh, yes. We *can*, at that. We were buskers on the street, we were, before we became robbers," explained Casper.

The barber handed him his clarinet: "Play a little, let me hear," he said.

"I can't play on one like that," said Casper. "But I can play the bassoon, if you know what that is."

"And Jesper plays the flute," said Jonathan.

"And Jonathan plays taps and drums or whatever else he can find to bang on," said Jesper.

"But then you're able to make up a whole orchestra," said barber Patterson.

"No, we *can't* do that, because we don't have our instruments any more," said Casper.

"We sold them for fifty-seven pounds," said Jesper.

"That was pretty daft," said Jonathan.

But now barber Patterson's interest was aroused: "If I can find you a bassoon and a flute and some drums, can you still play them?" he asked.

"Yes, I think I can say we probably can," said Casper.

"Then I shall see to it," said barber Patterson. And off he went into town to sort out some instruments.

While the barber was away, Mrs Bastian brought in some lunch. She had a real surprise when she saw the robbers with their hair parted and groomed. "Oh my, oh my, how handsome you all look," she exclaimed.

"Yes, we don't look too bad," said Casper. And then they all had a good laugh.

A little later that day barber Patterson returned, bringing with him drums and cymbal and flute and bassoon. "Now we have an orchestra," he said, although he was still not quite convinced the robbers could really play.

But he needn't have worried. Casper was so happy to be able to borrow the big bassoon, he patted it as if greeting a familiar friend, and tried out a few notes.

"This is just like the one I had when we were buskers," he said.

And Jesper held the flute aloft, peered into it and said: "Just the same here, too!" And he blew a few trills on the flute.

"You really do play, I can tell!" said barber Patterson enthusiastically.

"Oh yes, we do," said Casper. "And as soon as Jonathan's set up his drums and taps we'll play you a really authentic buskers' march—and it's a march composed by me—Casper. It dates from the time I was a street busker."

Then they began to play Casper's March, and barber Patterson was so enthusiastic he couldn't keep still. He gave a hop and a skip every time Jonathan tapped on the drums.

"Bravo, bravo, bravo!" he shouted.

And Police Inspector Bastian rushed in, too, when he heard the splendid music. "This is certainly a surprise," he beamed. And barber Patterson said eagerly: "You'll have to teach me that march, then I can teach it to grocer Hill and Anderson and drummer Parker. And we can play it at next year's Cardamom fête."

"We know another good one," said Casper. "It's a waltz, and if the barber cares to dance or do as you did before, then this is just the thing for dancing. Listen!"

The robbers played, and now barber Patterson was even more enthusiastic, and he wanted them to teach him the waltz straight away.

"We'd be glad to," said Casper, "you've been a wonderful barber and the right man for our hair."

"I think we'll have to wait till tomorrow," said Jesper, "because I have to go now."

"Is Jesper going?" asked barber Patterson, bewildered.

"Yes," said Bastian, "he has to take some food to a hungry lion. He should have been gone a while ago."

"But I'd love to play some more tomorrow," said Jesper, "and then we can teach you the whole march, as well as the waltz."

CHAPTER SEVENTEEN—THE LION EATS TOO MUCH—AND BASTIAN HAS AN IDEA

Jesper was let out of jail. He set off for the robbers' house with the sack on his back, the sack with the lion feed. It was a long walk, and he was late on this particular day. As he drew near the robbers' house he could hear the lion was a bit cross.

But the lion didn't have any reason to be cross, because it had everything a lion could want. The door to the little walled courtyard stood open, and the lion could stay out there as much as it liked. And at night—or when the weather was bad—all it had to do was to go into the bedroom and lie down on the bed.

Now it was pacing about, just inside the entrance, waiting for Jesper, and when Jesper opened up and went in with the sack of lion feed, the lion nearly knocked him off his feet.

"Down, Leo, down! No need to play so rough. Let me get the food out of the sack first," said Jesper. He unwrapped the deli-

118

cious meat dish and fetched a pail of water for the lion. And for pudding the lion had a bar of dairy milk chocolate from Police Inspector Bastian.

Before long the lion seemed well contented, and Jesper gave him a scratch behind the ears, because it liked that so much. "It's really rather a pity for you, Leo, that you didn't get arrested too," said Jesper. "But there's nothing to be done. You'll have to stay here for the time being, until the three of us are allowed home again. But now I have to go back to jail, otherwise Mr Bastian might get annoyed. Cheerio, enjoy yourself."

Then Jesper locked up and set off back to town.

Barber Patterson often called in at the jail for a chat and a quick jam, and to learn the robbers' new march and waltz. And *he* taught the robbers his hurrah march and other songs. Police Inspector Bastian and Mrs Bastian enjoyed the music just as much as the others. The police station was fairly jumping. Almost every day seemed like a fête.

But there was another matter that became more and more difficult for Police Inspector Bastian. Finding enough lion feed every day. The lion ate such an awful lot it was no wonder the pork butcher had to go sparingly on the meat.

"The pork butcher isn't able to let us have any more meat for the moment," Bastian said to Casper and Jesper and Jonathan one day.

"That's a pity," said Jesper.

"Yes," said Bastian, "I think we'll have to find another way to get lion feed."

"Perhaps we can *rob* someone," said Jonathan, quite forgetting himself. But Police Inspector Bastian responded angrily: "OH NO!" he said, "*no more robberies!*"

"No, that's right," said Jonathan.

"Perhaps we could go round the street busking," said Casper.

Then Police Inspector Bastian had a bright idea: "I know," he said. "You'll give a street buskers' concert in the square! Then people can pay a little to listen, and then there'll be money for the lion feed."

"That's a bright idea," said barber Patterson.

"Are you sure people will pay to hear us?" asked Jonathan.

"No doubt about it," reassured Bastian. And off he went to organize the concert.

Next day a bill was posted in the square. In large letters it read: "Concert in Aid of a Hungry Lion in the Square Today at Eight O'Clock. The Cardamom Prison Orchestra Will Play: 1. 'Casper's March'. 2. 'The Street Buskers' Waltz'. 3. 'The Hurrah March'. Adults: 20 pence—Children: 5 pence. A Once Only Event Not To Be Missed. Bastian—Superintendent."

All day long people passed by, and paused—and read what was written on the poster. And by six o'clock that evening the square was packed out with grown ups and little ones. There was Tobias and Aunt Sophia and the school master and grocer Hill and the pork butcher and Tommy and Remo and little Camomilla and many, many more. And Police Inspector Bastian, who was Master of Ceremonies, stepped forward and announced:

"A hearty good evening to one and all. Welcome to this very special, unique concert. It's wonderful so many of you have come, because it means we now have enough money to buy lion feed. And here's our Orchestra: This is Casper, who plays bassoon—and Jesper, who plays flute—and then this is Jonathan, who plays drums and cymbal. The first item on the programme is 'Casper's March'—and it's Casper himself who composed the music."

The orchestra played beautifully, beautifully—first Casper's March and afterwards the waltz—and, to finish, the Hurrah March, which barber Patterson had taught them.

So the concert came to a close, and the whole audience thought it had been a most entertaining evening. And when Police Inspector Bastian and Mrs Bastian counted up the takings, the total came to twenty-four pounds and fifty pence. All to go towards lion feed.

CHAPTER EIGHTEEN—A FIRE IN OLD TOBIAS'S TOWER—CASPER AND JESPER AND JONATHAN ACT COURAGEOUSLY

In the past, Tobias had felt somewhat lonely up in his tower. But he didn't feel like that any more. He had the little puppy, given to him by Remo. And he had Polly the parrot, given to him on his seventy-fifth birthday—to whom he could talk and who could answer him back. And Polly was a talkative parrot. Talking and talking and talking—and when Polly had nothing more to talk about, there was always the song about being a polly.

Yes, that Polly. A remarkably clever parrot, for sure. Tobias grew more and more fond of it each day. And the three of them had a fine time together.

But one day a dreadful thing happened. Old Tobias had gone to the pork butcher's to buy some meat produce, and the animals were at home on their own. All of a sudden the lower part of the tower house burst into flames. A passer-by who noticed smoke pouring out started to shout: "Fire!" And people came rushing to the rescue from all directions. Including Bastian and Silas and barber Patterson and many more.

Tobias himself came running back from the pork butcher's, and when he saw it was the tower house on fire he nearly collapsed. He shouted to everyone: "Is there anyone who can save my dog and my parrot—they're on their own up in the tower?"

There were many who tried, but they couldn't reach the top through the house because the lower part of the stairs was alight. The flames grew fiercer and fiercer, and they could hear the poor dog yelping high above.

"Oh, those poor animals!" cried Tobias in distress.

"Someone will have to climb up outside the house!" shouted Miss Sophia.

Then Police Inspector Bastian thought of Casper and Jesper and Jonathan. Robbers were bound to be experts at climbing up the outside of a house. He ran back to the police station, unlocked the cell door, and shouted to the robbers: "Casper, Jesper and Jonathan—hurry—up—quick, quick—the tower house is burning, and we need your help!"

"Depend on us, Mr Bastian," said Casper.

"We'll do our very best to help," said Jesper and Jonathan. They fairly leapt out of the cell and across to the site of the fire together with Police Inspector Bastian.

"Here come the three robbers," shouted Remo and Tommy and little Camomilla. And old Tobias shouted to the robbers: "Please, please, can you save my dog and my parrot, they're upstairs in the tower!"

"We'll do our best," answered Casper. And without more ado he began to clamber up the stone wall outside the house. Then he

had a thought. "Get a long rope!" he shouted down. And the baker jumped up and fetched the rope he'd used to tie the robbers with. "Here's the rope!" he shouted. Jesper grabbed the rope, and he and Jonathan clambered up after Casper, while the onlookers held their breath in the excitement.

"If only it's not too late," said old Tobias.

But Casper, already in reach of the balcony, swung himself over the balustrade and disappeared into the smoke filled tower. Jesper and Jonathan followed close on his heels.

"Look at those boys!" admired Police Inspector Bastian.

Everyone stood in suspense watching the top of the tower. Then suddenly little Camomilla cried: "There's the biggest of the robbers with the parrot cage!"

And sure enough, Casper came out of the smoke onto the platform above—holding the parrot cage in his hands. A moment later and Jesper was there too—cradling the puppy in his arms. And there, too, was Jonathan—with the telescope in one hand and Tobias's biscuit box in the other.

The square broke out in cheers. Everyone clapped and shouted hurrah, and Tobias tugged at his beard in delight.

"Look out down there!" shouted Casper. Then he hoisted down the parrot cage with the parrot in. And Polly was too terrified to say a word on the way down.

Old Tobias rushed forward and took hold of the cage. And then the rope was raised again. Next to be lowered were the precious telescope and the biscuit box, while the puppy had to wait till last, because it wasn't all that easy to secure him safely.

"He might slip out of the rope and fall down!" said Jonathan.

"Yes, but what'll we do then?" asked Casper.

"Better tie the rope round me," said Jesper.

So they did, and lowered Jesper down while he held the puppy safe and sound in his arms. They reached the ground in good shape, and Jesper handed the dog to old Tobias. Tobias was so relieved. He took Jesper by the hand and said: "You'll always be my closest friends!"

"We'd like to be," said Jesper.

So the dog and the parrot were rescued—and the telescope and the biscuit box as well. But Police Inspector Bastian was concerned about Casper and Jonathan. "You'll have to come down quickly before you're caught in the flames!" he shouted.

"No time," answered Casper. "We have to put the fire out first. Send up buckets of water!"

Now everyone joined in and helped. They fetched buckets and filled them with water—and the buckets were passed from person to person and on to Jesper. He hooked the buckets to the rope— one at a time—and Jonathan hoisted them up—and Casper ran into the tower with the buckets and emptied the water over the burning staircase. And Jonathan hoisted—and Casper emptied—they hoisted and emptied—and hoisted and emptied.

At first the smoke began to billow, but before long it gradually died away. And many buckets of water later, the fire was finally extinguished.

"That's enough," shouted Casper, "the fire's out!"

There was jubilation on the ground below, because everyone thought the job was so well done.

"Three cheers for the three robbers! Hurrah . . .!" they shouted.

Casper and Jonathan started to climb down again. And when they reached the ground, Old Tobias took Casper's hand and said: "You're the best fireman I've ever seen!"

"Talking of firemen," said Police Inspector Bastian, "we could certainly do with a fireman here in Cardamom Town. It's ridiculous the town doesn't have a fire officer!"

On hearing that, everyone shouted in agreement: "We want Casper for fire officer! We want Casper for fire officer!"

"Yes, that would be pretty sensible all round," said Bastian. "Would you like to take it on?" he asked Casper.

"That's what I've always wanted to do," said Casper.

"Then it's settled," affirmed Bastian. "As from today, Casper is fire officer for Cardamom Town!"

"I suppose we'll have to go back to jail now, won't we?" said Jesper and Jonathan.

"You can go wherever you like," said Bastian, "because you're no longer under arrest. You're free."

"Are we *completely* free?" asked Jesper and Jonathan.

"Completely free," said Bastian, nodding and smiling.

"Can we walk down the street like other folk?" asked Jesper.

"Just like other folk," said Bastian.

"We ought to try that," said Jonathan, "come on lads, let's take a stroll."

And so the three friends took a little jaunt round the square. They greeted everyone they met: "Good day, good day!" they said.—And everyone was friendly to them in return.

"This is a treat," said Casper.

"Yes—this is what it's like to be ordinary people," said Jesper happily.

They also came across Miss Aunt Sophia. That made them a bit apprehensive, and Jesper and Jonathan wanted to turn round and go another way, but Casper said: "Wait a moment—we have to be polite, remember! And, anyway, it's not certain she's going to be angry today."

And Casper greeted her politely, doffed his hat and said: "Good day, Miss Sophia. And please excuse us for carrying you off that time."

"Oh yes. Yes, yes.—Actually, I quite liked you all," said Sophia.

Jonathan was glad to hear that: "In fact, we liked you too— very much," he said.

"And you were truly courageous today," said Aunt Sophia.

"Oh," said Casper, "we can be more courageous than that."

"Especially Casper," said Jonathan. "And today he's been appointed fire officer for Cardamom Town."

"He'll make an excellent fire officer," said Sophia.

Then the baker came over. "Excuse me for interrupting," he said, "but I don't suppose one of you would care to join me as a baker. People eat so much bread and cake these days I can't manage to bake enough for everyone."

"That has to be Jonathan," said Casper, "because he's so amazingly fond of cakes."

"Me—Jonathan—am *I* to be a baker?" asked Jonathan.

"If you'd like to be," said the baker.

"That's what I've always wanted to be, for as long as I can remember," said Jonathan.

"You'll get a good wage," said the baker, "and you can eat as much cake as you want."

"Baker," said Jonathan, "can I start straight away?"

"You certainly can."

"Congratulations, Jonathan," said Aunt Sophia.

"We should be off to find Police Inspector Bastian and Mrs

Bastian to tell them, because they'll be very glad to hear about this."

"Say hallo from me," said Miss Sophia.

Police Inspector Bastian and Mrs Bastian were still over at the tower house when Casper and Jesper and Jonathan came by.

"Mr Bastian," said Casper, "Jonathan's found work!"

"He's going to be a baker," said Jesper.

"That's absolutely splendid news," said Mrs Bastian and Bastian.

"Yes, *that* it is," said Jonathan. "And when the Police Inspector himself, or Mrs Bastian, next has a birthday—come that day, greetings will arrive in the shape of a magnificent and delicious layer cake from baker Jonathan. You can count on it!"

"We look forward to that with pleasure," said Mrs Bastian.

But Jesper felt a little uncertain about the future, and what he might do. "Yes, Casper's a fireman, now, and Jonathan's a baker, but what's going to happen to me?" he said.

"What would you like to be, most of all?" asked Bastian.

"No—I don't dare say it," said Jesper.

"Just say it," said Mrs Bastian, "perhaps it can be arranged."

"It's so embarrassing," said Jesper.

"You can say it, Jesper," said Casper.

And Jesper looked down and said shyly: "I've—always— wanted to—be a circus ringmaster and director!"

"Yes, but a circus ringmaster and director is a splendid thing," said Bastian. "And it's a shame a town like Cardamom doesn't have a good circus," said Mrs Bastian.

"Yes, I think it's a shame," said Casper.

"I already have a lion, you know," said Jesper happily. "It would be good to have in a circus, because it's both clever and cuddly."

"Perhaps Pontius and me can join the circus as well?" said Tommy. "Pontius knows lots of circus tricks already."

"And we'll help you in the evenings and be circus musicians," said Casper.

"And then we can play the Casper March, because it would make a good circus march," said Jonathan.

And all ended well in the little town. Now there are no longer any robbers. Casper's become fire officer—and before long he'll be happily married. I'm not saying to whom—but it's to a lady who's good at keeping things tidy.

Jonathan's become a baker and he helps the baker to bake bread and cakes. And Jesper's become the circus director and ringmaster with a silk top hat and a lion. And everyone in town joins in singing the hurrah song which tram driver Puddleson wrote the day after the fire in the tower house.

HURRAH SONG FOR THE ROBBERS

We will sing our hurrah song and play
    hurrah hurrah
for those three who were rogues yesterday
    hurrah hurrah!
Now those three they are free—as we show,
    as we show,
for they no longer rob—as we know—
    as we know.
They have the most courageous names,
they clambered up and quenched the flames.
We will sing out hurrah and hallo!
    Hurrah hurrah!

And one's become fireman first grade
    hurrah hurrah!
wears a jacket with fine golden braid
    hurrah hurrah!
We've a circus whose number one draw
    biggest draw
is the lion we know from before
    from before.
And now Jonathan's a baker,
he's a butter cookie maker
baking sweet petits fours we adore
    hurrah hurrah!

CARDAMOM LYRICS AND MUSIC

THE CARDAMOM TRAM
AND THE CARDAMOM SONG

English words: Barnett

Original words and music: Egner

In the town of Cardamom our life is free from care. Here there are no cars, but there's a tram for every fare. I'm the tram conductor on the line called number one, direction north to south is how we run. We start off every quarter hour, (bell) there's room to carry many more. And by the bridge is where we stop, we turn the tram round at the top. And if you want to ride straight back, just climb the stair beside the door, for you can ride the upper deck, and see the sights when there's no shower. Now all are seated we'll depart (bell) and now our tram can make a start.

POLICE INSPECTOR BASTIAN'S SONG

English words : Barnett

Original words and music : Egner

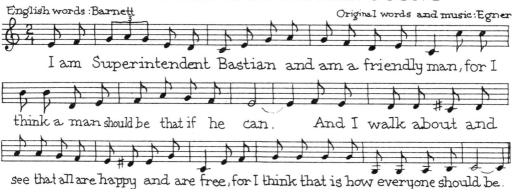

I am Superintendent Bastian and am a friendly man, for I
think a man should be that if he can. And I walk about and
see that all are happy and are free, for I think that is how everyone should be.

THE WEATHER SONG

English words : Barnett

Original words and music : Egner

When it's close to harvest feast, and the wind blows from the east, then the
rain comes pouring down everywhere upon the town. And in Cardamom high street under
cover people meet if they do not have galoshes on their feet.

THE ROBBERS' SONG

English words : Barnett

Original words and music : Egner

We sneak on tiptoe as we go so stealthily to steal-o. We
take just what we need and know where we can find a meal-o. Now darkness lies u-
pon the town, asleep beneath its eiderdown. We're off with our bag and our
bucket and pan, both Casper and Jesper and Jonathan.

CAMOMILLA PLAYS

English words: Barnett

Original words and music: Egner

Hear me in my forte play my pianoforte-one and two and three and one and two and three. I am counting right and reading notes by sight and- one and two and three and- one and two and three. One and two and three.

After last verse:

AUNT SOPHIA'S ANGRY SONG

English words: Barnett

Original words and music: Egner

O fiddlesticks o fiddlesticks, I'm angry and I'll frown! It's stuff and nonsense everywhere in Cardamom our town. If only people were like me –it would be very good. But no one is at all like me - they don't do what they should.

HORSE DANCE

English words: Barnett

Original words and music: Egner

Trip the light fantastic with four legs down and tail high - hey ho hop Hippo - crates. Chest pushed out and belly taut and supple limbs will fly - hey ho hop Hippocrates. Bare your lovely teeth -and turn your head a bit askew. Watch the steps I take and try to follow what I do. Afterwards there's sugar lumps and timothy grass to chew-hey ho hop Hippocrates.

THE TALKING CAMEL

English words : Barnett

Original words
and music : Egner

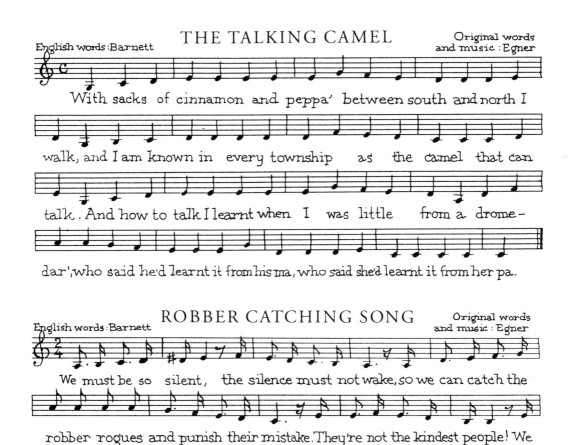

With sacks of cinnamon and peppa' between south and north I

walk, and I am known in every township as the camel that can

talk . And how to talk I learnt when I was little from a drome-

dar', who said he'd learnt it from his ma, who said she'd learnt it from her pa.

ROBBER CATCHING SONG

English words : Barnett

Original words
and music : Egner

We must be so silent, the silence must not wake, so we can catch the

robber rogues and punish their mistake. They're not the kindest people! We

want a quick arrest . For each is just a rascal like every robber pest.

THE ROBBERS' LOOKING SONG

Original words
and music : Egner

English words : Barnett

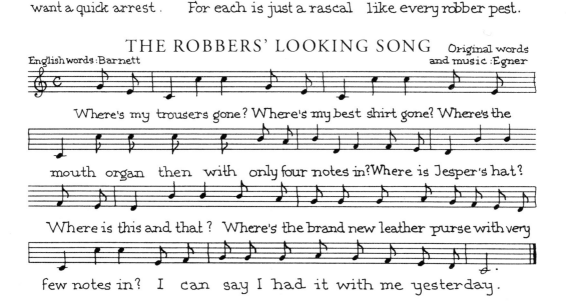

Where's my trousers gone? Where's my best shirt gone? Where's the

mouth organ then with only four notes in? Where is Jesper's hat?

Where is this and that ? Where's the brand new leather purse with very

few notes in? I can say I had it with me yesterday.

137

THE ROBBERS' WASHING SONG

English words: Barnett

Original words and music: Egner

To wash ourselves-that's the most unpleasant yet. Brushes are too rough, and water is too wet.

No, scrub and brush, soap and waterpan are nothing proper for a robber man.

THE PRETTY POLLY FROM AMERICA

English words: Barnett

Original words and music: Egner

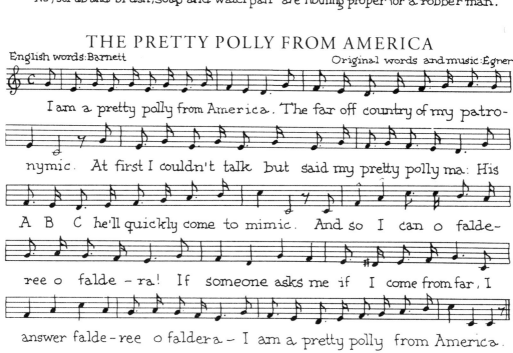

I am a pretty polly from America. The far off country of my patro-

nymic. At first I couldn't talk but said my pretty polly ma: His

A B C he'll quickly come to mimic. And so I can o falde-

ree o falde-ra! If someone asks me if I come from far, I

answer falde-ree o faldera - I am a pretty polly from America.

HURRAH SONG

English words: Barnett

Original words and music: Egner

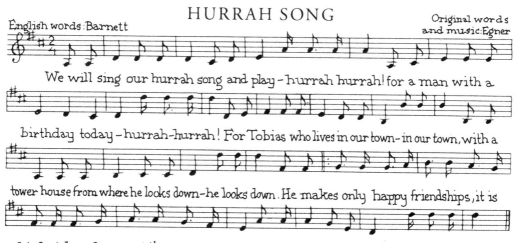

We will sing our hurrah song and play-hurrah hurrah! for a man with a

birthday today-hurrah-hurrah! For Tobias who lives in our town-in our town, with a

tower house from where he looks down-he looks down. He makes only happy friendships, it is

his hat he always tips when he greets everyone in our town - hurrah hurrah!

MRS BASTIAN'S SONG

English words: Barnett

Original words and music: Egner

I tidy and I straighten and keep things spick and span. And Superintendent Bastian – he is the sweetest man. My husband really is a peach, he is so kind and fair, and when I do the washing up, the drying is his share.

THE MASTER BARBER'S SONG

English words: Barnett

Original words: Egner ; music: Amdahl

I wash and cut and shape the hair of townsfolk all day long. But most of all I like to play a music singalong. In Cardamom Town Orchestra I am the leading man, and try to play my clarinet as often as I can. (Clarinet solo:)